'You're awful  boss,'

Noah said. 'I coul

'You don't scare me,' Olivia replied.

'Really?' Noah leaned in closer, irresistibly drawn by her saucy grin. 'And why is that?'

'If you were as mean as you want me to think you are, you never would have come back for me at that bus station.'

He wondered what she would say if she knew it had not been only kindness that had caused him to extend his help. More important, however, he wondered what she would do if he tasted that rosebud of a mouth she was lifting towards his.

'I'm not really so nice,' he murmured.

Her eyes had gone all soft. 'I think you are nice. Very nice.'

He kissed her then, before he could come to his senses. He kissed her, even as he was damning his foolishness to hell.

Dear Reader,

Welcome to Silhouette Special Edition®!

Our THAT'S MY BABY! title for this month is *Maternal Instincts* by Beth Henderson, a charming story where the heroine was just hoping to get a little experience with a baby, and ends up taking on the single dad, too!

There's also a baby on the way in the final one of Muriel Jensen's novels about identical triplets, *Father Found*, and in Penny Richards' intense and dramatic *Judging Justine*.

We are always pleased to announce another book from top-notch writer Sherryl Woods and *The Delacourt Scandal* is not only the latest in her AND BABY MAKES THREE series, it's her fiftieth book, too!

We're also delighted to have fabulous books from veteran writers Victoria Pade (*The Cowboy's Gift-Wrapped Bride*) and Celeste Hamilton (*Her Wildest Wedding Dreams*). No prizes for guessing which one is set at Christmas!

Please do enjoy them all.

The Editors

PS Don't forget to look for the new Superromances this month—there are wonderful new books from Cathy Gillen Thacker and Muriel Jensen, *and* two terrific Christmas stories, too!

Her Wildest
Wedding Dreams

CELESTE
HAMILTON

SILHOUETTE®
SPECIAL EDITION™

Silhouette, Silhouette Special Edition and Colophon are registered trademarks of Harlequin Books S.A., used under licence.

First published in Great Britain 2001
Silhouette Books, Eton House, 18-24 Paradise Road,
Richmond, Surrey TW9 1SR

© Jan Hamilton Powell 2000

ISBN 0 373 24319 7

23-1201

Printed and bound in Spain
by Litografia Rosés S.A., Barcelona

CELESTE HAMILTON

has been writing since she was ten years old, with the encouragement of parents who told her she could do anything she set out to do and teachers who helped her refine her talents.

The media captured her interest at school, and she graduated from the University of Tennessee with a degree in Communications. From there, she began writing and producing commercials at a Chattanooga, Tennessee, radio station.

Celeste began writing romances in 1985 and now works at her craft full-time. Married to a policeman, she likes nothing better than spending time at home with him and their two much-loved cats, although she and her husband also enjoy travelling when their busy schedules permit. Wherever they go, however, 'It's always nice to come home to East Tennessee—one of the most beautiful corners of the world.'

For 'The Loop': Marcy Froemke, Faith Garner, Janice Maynard, Jan McDaniel, Lurlene McDaniel, Leigh Neely, Susan Sawyer and Clara Wimberly. For reasons they understand.

Chapter One

Olivia Franklin knew no bride-to-be could ask for a more beautiful setting for a prenuptial bash. A breeze softened the late-May evening. The sun had slipped past the western horizon, painting the big, Texas sky in pinks and lavenders, hues echoed by the pansies and petunias edging the tiled patio. A string quartet accompanied the laughter of the guests and the tinkling of ice in fine crystal.

Groups strolled in and out of the stucco mansion and wandered from the veranda to the buffet set up in a tent on the lawn. The movers and shakers of Austin were out in glittering force to toast the wedding of Roger Franklin's daughter.

That's all she was to them. *Roger Franklin's daughter.*

Soon to be Marshall Crane's wife.

Olivia set her champagne flute on a table and walked, virtually unnoticed, around the periphery of the crowd. At the other end of the veranda, her father held court. Marshall stood beside him, smiling as Roger clapped him on the shoulder and grinned his approval. Tomorrow, when Marshall said "I do" to Olivia, he would become much more than just her father's business protégé. He would be family. Roger would have exactly what he wanted. So would Marshall.

And what about her?

Olivia found it difficult to breathe.

She went into the house and made her way upstairs, nodding and murmuring excuses to the few who sought to detain her. How ironic. She was supposed to be the evening's honored guest. The bride. But she could slip away almost undetected.

An excited bark greeted her as she closed her bedroom door. A tiny ball of fur streaked from the bed and began a dance around Olivia's feet. She knelt and gathered her Yorkshire terrier into her arms. "Hello, Puddin', baby. Hello, sweet girl."

A sniff brought Olivia to her feet, still holding the dog. In the doorway to her dressing room, a mountain of a woman stood with a stack of clothing in her arms. Mary Gunter's broad face registered her disapproval, and she addressed Olivia with the familiarity of over twenty years as nurse, maid and surrogate mother. "What are you doing up here?"

"No one cares if I'm at the party or not." Olivia's bronze silk skirt swished about her ankles as she stalked across the room. Puddin' gave her a comforting lick on the chin.

Mary carefully tucked clothing into one of several suitcases open on the bed. "Poor little girl," she said in a singsong voice, just as she might have when Olivia was ten. "All alone and feeling sorry for herself."

The woman's persistence in treating her like a child was a long-running battle Olivia couldn't face right now. Pausing at one of the windows beside her bed, Olivia drew back a sheer panel. Her room overlooked the side of the house closest to the barns and stables, away from the gardens and the party, but she could still hear the music and laughter. "All of those people are here to see Father. They don't care about me."

"Now, now…"

"It's true." Idly Olivia watched a truck with a camper and a horse trailer turn off the main drive and down the road toward the barns.

"You're being silly."

The truck and camper drew to a stop at the stables, and with a sigh Olivia turned back to Mary. "I'm just the great man's daughter. Not a great beauty like her mother. Not a genius like her father. Nothing too spectacular at all. A mere curiosity worth only a glance or two because I've been kept under lock and key most of my life."

"Your father has tried to protect you. You know why." The rebuke in Mary's tone was clear.

Olivia bit her lip to stop her flippant retort. Of course she knew her father's reasons. An electronics whiz kid, Roger Franklin had started his own company while still in his twenties. A millionaire by thirty-five, he married the most sought-after debutante in Austin. Fifteen years ago, when Olivia was only eight, her mother had been kidnapped. Roger had paid the ransom, but beautiful Leila Franklin was killed. Roger had never stopped blaming himself or striving to keep his and Leila's only child safe.

Much of the time Olivia had been able to forgive her father his overprotectiveness. Though she had often felt like an unbroken horse kicking at the door of a stall, she had done as her father had asked. She agreed to the bodyguards who accompanied her everywhere, to school, shopping, on infrequent excursions with schoolmates or dates. She lived at the family town house in Austin instead of a dormitory or apartment while she attended college. She set aside her desire to use her artistic talents and start a career. Her father wouldn't even consider her working in his own company.

The reason she knew few of the people at tonight's party was because he wanted it that way. He had discouraged friendships. Olivia had found friends despite him, especially during college. However, most of those friends were busy leading lives that didn't include guards and gates and fences. Olivia spent most of her time here at the ranch, where her father often entertained. She played hostess, but never became really close to any of their guests.

To some people she led an idyllic life. No worries about money. A beautiful home. Gorgeous clothes. Prize-winning horses. A pool and tennis courts. A staff to see to her every need. Travel to exotic destinations whenever her father deemed it suitable.

Olivia had tried very hard to see herself as lucky.

When her father had first pushed her to go out with Marshall, she had been surprised. And then grateful. For with Marshall, she had actually seen a way out of her gilded cage. With a man her father trusted, surely she could begin to live her own life.

Marshall was easy to like—good-looking, educated, a pleasant companion. He sympathized with Olivia's desire for independence. She never once deluded herself into thinking she loved the man, but she found him kind and attentive. They shared interests in horses, in music and books. Olivia had looked forward to moving into his home when they returned from their month-long European honeymoon. She had imagined them living a pleasant, normal life. Surely, as a married woman who managed her own affairs, she would finally escape the shadows of fear which had haunted her father and enslaved her.

But this afternoon Marshall had informed her they would be living here. With the security cameras outside. With the guard at the gate. With someone watching her every move. When she had protested, Marshall had reminded her that here she was safe.

Safe? More like trapped.

He had sounded just like her father.

This afternoon Olivia had realized she saw her marriage *only* as an escape, a way out of the luxurious prison of her life. Before today, she had convinced herself she really wanted to make a life with Marshall. Now she saw he was prepared to join her father as an additional prison guard. And that was no life at all.

' All day she had entertained fantasies of running away. Of kicking over the tables of wedding gifts downstairs and racing out the front door. Of stealing one of the caterer's uniforms and sliding anonymously out the kitchen entrance. Of mingling with the guests, getting into a car and driving away.

But all she could think of were the times she had tried to escape. To an afternoon alone at the movies with a friend from school. For a weekend with her one-and-only boyfriend before Marshall. Or in Paris last year, when she simply wanted to walk down a legendary street with the knowledge that she was truly on her own. Her father's men had found her. They had always found her.

Her father regarded these attempts at independence as indications of Olivia's immaturity. He called her impulsive and naive, and made her feel foolish and none too intelligent. At the same time, he said he loved her and wanted to protect her.

Maybe that's why Olivia couldn't hate him, even when he made her feel so inadequate. He truly believed he was saving her as he had been unable to save her mother. The people who had kidnapped Leila had been hired to work here at the ranch. Roger had trusted them, let them into his family's lives, and they had betrayed him. Since then his vigilance had never wavered. It never would.

Once more Olivia found she couldn't breathe.

"Are you okay?"

Glancing up to meet Mary's concerned gaze, Olivia managed to draw in and release a breath. "I'm just...excited..."

"Of course you are." Smiling, Mary turned toward the corner where a shimmering dress of satin and tulle hung in front of a three-paneled mirror. "Tomorrow, you'll wear your mother's dress, walk down the aisle at the church, dance at the reception at the country club, and you'll be the most beautiful bride Austin has ever seen. Mr. Roger and Mr. Marshall will be so proud. Those people downstairs will never forget you."

Yes, she would be memorable. As Roger Franklin's daughter. Marshall Crane's bride. They would never know Olivia Kay Franklin. No one was allowed to know her. She wasn't even sure she knew herself.

Puddin' gave a startled *yip* just as the door banged open. Roger Franklin strode into the room, and the dog leaped to the floor to greet him.

Olivia's father wasn't a tall man. No more than average height, he was stout of build and not handsome by any stretch of imagination. His red hair, which Olivia had inherited, had gone gray at the temples. His brown eyes, also like hers, flashed in a face unremarkable of feature. But what Roger Franklin lacked in looks, he made up for in presence. He exuded power, confidence and strength.

As was often the case, Olivia resisted an impudent temptation to salute him. "Hello, Father."

"You should be downstairs."

"I know."

"Then why aren't you?"

"I needed to get away for a few minutes."

"Marshall wants you at his side."

"Does he?" Hard as she tried, Olivia could not keep the sarcasm out of her voice. Once she might have been pleased to think she was needed at her fiancé's side, but now that charade seemed foolish.

Her father lifted an eyebrow. "Is there something wrong, Olivia?"

Only everything, she wanted to say. But what would that prove? Instead, she shook her head.

At Roger's feet, Puddin' jumped and yapped, begging for his attention. Olivia had seen her father indulge her pampered pet, who was not the least bit intimidated by the man, but now he snapped, "Could you make her hush, Olivia?"

She picked up the dog, but Puddin' continued to whimper, her soulful black eyes fastened on Roger.

He sighed wearily. "Olivia, you should return to our party, especially since I need to step away for a while."

"Something wrong?"

He made an impatient gesture with one hand. "The breeder who is buying Royal Pleasure just arrived."

Mention of one of her favorite mounts sent a pang through Olivia. "Must you sell her?"

"She served her purpose."

The prize-winning Tennessee Walker had produced two colts sired by the cream of the Franklin stable. Now she was going to the highest bidder. Olivia felt a distinct kinship to the beautiful horse, who had no say in her own fate.

"Can't the breeder just deal with Jake?" Olivia asked, referring to her father's foreman. "Or wait until after the party?"

"You know I take care of these things myself. And there's no reason to wait. The breeder can be on his way with Royal Pleasure first thing in the morning."

"Of course," she murmured, feeling silly. Her father made his own deals, operated strictly hands-on, in control, on his own schedule. It had been suggested that he would be even richer, his company even more successful, if he would loosen the reins a bit. He scoffed at such suggestions.

"Come down to the party," Roger commanded.

"Just let me touch up my makeup."

Her father nodded, scowled down at Puddin' and reluctantly reached out and patted the dog's head. Shivers of delight erupted in the tiny dog's body.

Dryly Roger observed, "She's coating you in dog hair."

Glancing with dismay at her sheer white blouse, Olivia felt sixteen instead of twenty-three.

Roger started to turn away, then paused. His voice deepened. His harsh features softened somewhat. "You know you look like your mother tonight. Very lovely."

Olivia swallowed hard. She knew she was nothing like her elegant, blond mother, and couldn't imagine why her father mentioned any resemblance.

He continued, "She would be happy about this wedding. Just as I am. Marshall can take care of you."

Words stuck in Olivia's throat. The thought of being taken care of for the rest of her life was too terrible for comment.

Her father seemed to take her silence as agreement, for he nodded and strode out of the room.

Olivia sank down on the edge of the bed, anger pounding inside her.

I have to get out of here. I have to escape.

Puddin's protests and Mary's voice gradually penetrated the shouting in Olivia's brain.

"You must go," Mary murmured, regarding her with concern. "Go."

Slowly Olivia released her dog and looked up at her longtime nanny. "Yes," she agreed. "I must go."

She wasn't talking about returning to the party.

"Here, pretty lady. That's right. Right here." Noah Raybourne sighed his approval as he ran a hand down the mare's sleek, ebony coat. Royal Pleasure stomped her front legs and turned her regal head toward him, her breath rising like a cloud in the cool morning air.

The grizzled Franklin ranch boss, Jake Keneally, scratched his beard. ''It's almost as if she knows you.''

''Maybe she recognizes family.''

Jake peered at him in puzzlement.

''Her mama's sire belonged to my father,'' Noah explained, stroking the mare's velvety nose. ''Carmen's Best Boy was born and bred on Raybourne Farms. He was named for my mother.''

''I knew the horse,'' Jake replied. ''But he belonged to a breeder over toward Dallas.''

Familiar anger tightened Noah's gut. ''My stepfather sold him out from under us.''

The ranch boss apparently had enough firsthand knowledge of troubles to keep from prying. He grunted and gave Royal Pleasure a loving stroke of his own. ''I won't say I'm glad to see this beauty leave us, but it's good to hear she's going where she'll be appreciated.''

''That she will.'' Noah took Royal Pleasure's lead and walked her toward his horse trailer, talking gently to her all the while.

With a minimum of fuss, she was loaded aboard the white trailer emblazoned with an ornate *R* in black script.

Noah tossed his duffel bag on the front seat of his truck and turned to shake Jake's hand. ''Thanks for your help. I especially appreciate the grub and the comfortable bed last night.'' He gestured toward the camper on his truck bed. ''More than a few nights in this thing can get pretty old.''

With a final wave, Noah swung into the driver's seat and was on his way. The sun, though not yet visible, was lighting the eastern horizon as he stopped at the gate. A uniformed guard, different from the man he had seen last night, stepped up to the window with a clipboard in hand. ''Hello, Mr. Raybourne. Jake called to say you were headed out.''

''You folks take security seriously round here, don't you?'' Noah commented with a smile.

The guard gave him a steady, measuring look. ''Mr. Franklin is pretty clear about how he wants things handled.''

''I'm sure he is.'' Noah imagined Roger Franklin was crystal clear about all matters affecting his family, his business and holdings.

The guard made a notation on his clipboard, then stepped back and studied the truck and trailer for a moment. Apparently reassured there was no reason to conduct a search, he opened the automatic gate and waved Noah through.

The whole operation amused Noah. He understood that a rich man might have some security concerns, but this place was set up like a fortress. Maybe the extra precautions were in place because of that big party they had last night. Jake had told him Franklin's daughter was getting married today.

Peering at the golden glow on the horizon and at the sky, which was changing from gray to blue, Noah muttered, ''Looks like beautiful weather for a wedding.'' He met his own gaze in the rearview mirror. ''Sure hope it goes better than mine.''

If things had gone as planned, he and Amy would have celebrated their third anniversary a couple of weeks ago. Noah's mother had blamed the passage of that date on the foul mood that had gripped him of late. She was wrong, Noah told himself. He was well and truly over Amy. He had gotten beyond being left at the altar. Only rarely did he think about having to walk out into that church and announce to everyone that the girl he loved had changed her mind about hitching her star to a struggling horse breeder whose only debt-free asset was the fire burning in his belly.

Realizing he gripped the steering wheel with undue force, Noah made himself relax. Maybe his mother was right, after all. Perhaps his foul mood wasn't just the result of too much work and worry. He had been thinking about Amy. Her engagement to a successful Nashville businessman was announced last month. The news had started Noah questioning himself. Had what Amy wanted really been so wrong?

Before they were to marry, she had asked Noah to sell a half interest in his operation to her father. The capital would have provided Noah with the means to rebuild much of the farm and breeding business his irresponsible stepfather had tried to destroy. The money would also have allowed them to redo the farmhouse and live in the sort of comfort to which Amy was accustomed.

But Noah had wanted them to rebuild the farm themselves, as a team, working as his parents once had and as his grandparents before them. Though he knew Amy's father to be a good, honest man, he was fearful of letting an outsider have any say in the farm his grandfather had founded and his father had run so successfully. The only other outsider to interfere in Raybourne Farms had almost ruined it. Noah couldn't do what Amy asked.

She had called him a pigheaded, prideful fool, and they had argued. But he had still believed she loved him and intended to go through with the wedding. He had underestimated her fears about living on the limited means he had to offer. After all the other embarrassment his family had endured in the community, Noah still couldn't believe she had left him standing at the altar. But she had.

Her willingness to humiliate him in such a public way should have Noah thanking his lucky stars to have escaped marriage to her.

But on those days when he worked his body to weary numbness, when he faced a lonely night at home, when he awoke to an empty bed, Noah wasn't so sure he was lucky.

Struggling to clear the clouds of regret from his brain, he turned onto the main highway, heading east, toward home. He was going to avoid the high speeds of the interstate, keep to the secondary highways and stop as often as possible to stretch Royal Pleasure's legs. That beauty was an integral part of his plans for Raybourne Farms. She had cost him the better part of his bank balance, and he wasn't taking any chances with her.

The sun was fast revealing the East Texas landscape. He shook his head. Some people might find this land appealing, but he'd take the rolling green meadows of Middle Tennessee any day.

He rested his elbow on the open window. A squeak sounded from behind. Followed by another. And still another. He eased up on the accelerator and leaned back, listening intently, then peered in the side mirror for signs of trouble with the trailer. He saw nothing.

Once more Noah relaxed and began to whistle.

Hours passed before the squeak returned. Then grew in volume. And Noah recognized the sound for what it was—the insistent yapping of a dog.

"What the hell?" He carefully eased the truck and trailer off the road, got out and hurried around to throw open the door at the back of the truck.

He heard a shout of warning.

Something small and furry bounced against his chest, sending him stumbling against the trailer. Then something else barreled past Noah. It was a boy…no, those breasts and that rounded rear end were most definitely feminine. They belonged to a young woman. She was dressed in jeans, T-shirt and baseball cap and was calling, "Puddin', you stupid dog. Puddin'! Come here."

Noah straightened in time to peer around the truck and see the dog relieve itself in a patch of grass beside the road.

"Oh, Puddin'," the young woman crooned. Two long, red braids escaped from her cap as she stooped to stroke the little mutt's head. "I'm sorry, girl. I know you couldn't hold it another minute."

The dog barked up at her mistress, then raced around her and made straight for Noah. Looking like an animated ball of long, silky fur, she circled his boots, fussing at him in her squeaky, high-pitched bark.

Noah looked from dog to woman and back again. At any minute he expected a video camera to emerge from around the trailer and some smarmy TV personality to announce he was the subject of an elaborate scheme.

Instead, the young woman tugged on the brim of her baseball cap and darted nervous glances toward the highway, where a car swished past.

Noah began, "Who the hell are—"

The young woman cut him short by grabbing her dog and ducking between the trailer and the camper to the other side of the truck. "Let's get off the road!"

Noah had little choice but to follow. On the other side he caught hold of her arm. "What were you and this…" He glared at the dog, who peered up at him through its long hair, some of which was held back by silly, girlish hair bows. Useless creature, Noah thought, before returning to his demand, "What were you and this dog doing in my trailer?"

The stowaway offered a senseless explanation about mistaking his camper for her own, falling asleep and awakening when the dog started barking.

"You'll have to do better than that. What are you up to?" His eyes narrowed in suspicion. "Have you done something to my horse?"

He set her away from him and stalked around to throw open the doors to the spacious trailer. It made no sense that she could have gotten from the trailer to the camper without his knowledge, but he had to check.

Royal Pleasure whinnied and danced around a bit, but otherwise seemed just fine. Noah patted her reassuringly, then exited the trailer, eager for the explanation the redhead owed him. To his surprise she was hightailing it through the weeds beside the road, heading for a stand of trees nearby.

He was tempted to let her go. She had obviously been up to no good, stowing away in his camper like some little thief. She probably was a thief. The possibility made his blood run cold. Right now, she probably had something that belonged to Roger Franklin, a man who had his home barricaded like a castle keep. A man who might assume Noah was the real thief or in cahoots with her.

"Hey," Noah shouted as he sprinted after her. "You come back here."

She darted a glance over her shoulder but kept moving, her dog barking up a storm in her arms.

Overtaking her took only a few moments. She was such a little thing, Noah brought her to a halt simply by catching the hem of her T-shirt.

Brought round to face him, she pleaded, "Please just let me go. I didn't hurt anything. I just needed a ride."

"You needed to sneak off the Franklin ranch." Noah anchored her in place with a firm grip on her shoulders. "What are you running from?"

Her brown-eyed gaze wouldn't quite meet his. "I just had to get out of there."

"Why? What'd you steal?"

"Steal?" she sputtered. "You think I'm a thief?"

"Why else would you be running away like this?"

Olivia remained silent, desperately searching for an explanation.

The man gave her a little shake. "What is it? What are you running from?"

"My father." The words burst out of her without preamble or thought.

Her captor's blue eyes narrowed. "Your father?"

"I just can't stand it any longer. I had to get away from him."

The grip on her shoulders loosened somewhat. "Why? What's the problem with him?"

"He...just..." Olivia swallowed hard, not certain what to say. She was a terrible liar. The few times she had tried, she had been found out instantly. But somehow she had to convince this man to let her go. She doubted that would happen if he found out she was Roger Franklin's daughter. And if she had to go back now...

"What?" the stranger prompted.

Olivia's heart knocked hard against her chest as she struggled for words. She had come too far to mess up. Getting out of the house in the early hours of the morning had been a minor miracle. She had escaped through a window she had left open in the library, falling hard on her right arm and almost crushing poor Puddin'. But when no lights came on nor alarms sounded, she realized the security system wasn't fully engaged, possibly due to the party and the caterers who were still loading equipment and cleaning up near the kitchen entrance.

Aided by her knowledge of the outside security cameras and the schedule of the guards who patrolled the grounds each night, she had crept behind bushes on the perimeter of the yard and through the deepest of shadows to the stables.

Even then, she hadn't a clear plan as to how she would get off the ranch. She was considering saddling a horse and riding out when she had noticed the horse breeder's trailer. Remembering her father saying Royal Pleasure's new owner would be leaving first thing in the morning, she had taken what seemed like her best chance and stowed away. She had been hoping to sneak out of the camper when he stopped for gasoline or to exercise Royal Pleasure.

Bringing Puddin' had been a risk, and most likely a mistake. Yet leaving her only friend in the world had been impossible. Olivia couldn't do it. And truly, the dog had been so quiet, so good. Until she simply had to go to the bathroom.

The horse breeder still regarded her with open hostility. "I don't believe this nonsense about running from your father."

"But it's true," Olivia protested, relieved that she didn't have to lie. "I had to get away from him."

"He works for Franklin?"

"Yes...in...in the stables," she prevaricated. "As a trainer."

"And he hurt you?" An emotion that could have been sympathy flickered across the man's face.

"Yes, he hurt me." At least that much wasn't a lie, Olivia thought. Her father had hurt her.

"But why would you have to hide to get away?"

"My father would never willingly let me go."

Looking even more suspicious, one of her captor's hands slipped from her shoulder down her arm, the arm she had fallen on in her escape. Olivia winced and looked down. For the first time she noticed the purple bruise that started just below the hem of her sleeve.

The man saw it, too. Gently he pushed the sleeve up. The bruise stretched from near her elbow to her shoulder.

Muttering a curse, the man dropped her arm and stepped away. "Did your father do this to you?"

"He...he made me fall," Olivia said.

"He pushed you?"

She nodded.

The breeder peered at her again, clearly torn between believing and doubting her story. "How old are you?" he asked at last. "Over eighteen, I imagine."

"Yes."

"There's no reason why you couldn't just have left."

"You don't understand," she explained, feeling desperate. "My father, he's...nuts. I was so scared of him, so afraid."

"You could have told someone. Told Jake or Mr. Franklin."

She forced out a laugh. "You think a rich, important man like that would care about me?"

"Roger Franklin strikes me as a decent man. He'd care if one of his employees was beating his daughter."

"Yeah, he'd fire my father, and I'd get blamed."

"No, you would have gotten help." The breeder shook his head. "There's some other reason you're running." He took hold of her uninjured arm. "Come on back to the truck. We're going to find a telephone and call the ranch."

Olivia struggled to free herself, her eyes filling with tears. In her arms Puddin' whined. She could not go back. The very fact that they had made it this far meant she had something of a head start.

"Please," she begged. "Please believe me. I have to get away from my father. I can't stand it any longer. Please." Olivia didn't want to break down completely, but hysteria rose inside her. She fought the sobs and started to tremble.

"Jeez." The breeder's forehead creased, and he thrust a hand through wavy, light-brown hair. "You really are scared to death, aren't you?"

Olivia nodded while Puddin' licked her trembling chin.

The man stared at her hard for a few moments more while she struggled to bring herself under control. He seemed like a kind person. Handsome in a strong, hard-planed sort of way. Clearly he sympathized with her somewhat, else he would have already hauled her back to the camper and locked her in.

Olivia focused on playing on that sympathy. "I'm so…sorry I hid in your camper. I'm not a thief. I just need a break. Please. Just drive away and leave us here. Please."

Noah was tempted to do just that. Something told him this young woman wasn't a thief. But something in her story didn't strike him as quite right, either. The best thing he could do for himself was get in the truck and drive away.

And that's exactly what he was going to do.

"You've got a deal, little lady. If anybody ever asks me, I'll tell them I've never seen you before." He jerked a thumb over his shoulder, toward the truck. "You got anything in the camper?"

"A small bag."

He swung the door wide open and retrieved a small, and to his admittedly inexperienced eye, expensive-looking tote bag. He thought about searching it for stolen jewelry, but decided he didn't want to know if she was hiding something. He just wanted to get back on the road.

He rooted in a cooler and found two bottled waters. Outside, he handed everything over to her. "Here you go."

She swiped at the tears on her cheeks before taking the bag and the water. "Thank you so much. I'm sorry I've delayed you. You've really been so kind."

Her choice of words didn't strike Noah as those of a stable hand's daughter. Determinedly, he slammed the door on his doubts. Giving her a little salute, he went around the trailer to make sure the door was secured. He closed and locked the camper door, as well, then climbed into the truck.

His stowaway had moved just ahead of him on the road, where she struggled to fit the water bottles into her bag while holding on to her dog. She looked small and awkward.

Noah's conscience pinched him hard.

He leaned out the window. "You be careful."

"I will," she shouted back.

He waved. He even started the truck. But he didn't move.

Ahead of him, she started walking. Her determined

strides did nothing to disguise the downright tempting curves of her behind.

"Just let her go," Noah told his reflection in the mirror.

And leave her and that useless dog alone on this stretch of highway?

"They'll be just fine."

If they don't meet up with a rattlesnake.

"A snake would run the other way."

But some pervert in a rusted-out pickup just might want a piece of her cute little butt.

Noah closed his eyes for a moment, trying not to think about that bruise on her arm or her tears when she said she'd been hurt by her father. God knew, he understood that kind of pain. He just wished his dear mother had not worked so hard to instill a sense of honor in him. Finally he let out a long breath, eased the truck into drive and leaned out the window, calling, "Hey, come here."

She hurried up to the window. The hope mingling with fear on her face was more than he could stand.

"All right," he muttered. "I've got this terrible feeling that I'm going to regret this, but here's what we're going to do. First, you get in the truck."

She frowned, as if she didn't understand him.

"Get in the truck, and at the next town you can catch a bus somewhere." She gave him a blank look. "You do want to get on a bus or something, don't you? There was some destination in mind when you set out on this little trip?"

Though she nodded, her expression gave her away.

"She has no idea where she's going," he muttered as she came around to the passenger side. "No clue. Just her and that damn dog, tearing off like Dorothy and Toto on the yellow brick road."

"Thank you, thank you, thank you," she gushed as she climbed in beside him. "I was willing to walk, but this will be so much quicker and easier."

The dog jumped onto the seat, then leaped up and licked Noah's cheek.

He groaned. The dog barked and tried for a second lick.

"Just keep the mutt under control," Noah ordered.

She pulled the dog onto her lap. "Her name's Puddin'."

"And your name?"

She hesitated. Briefly. But long enough for Noah to figure she was lying. "Libby. Libby Kay."

"I'm Noah," he said, offering a handshake. The hand she placed in his was soft as silk, with nails finely manicured. Not exactly the hands of a working man's daughter.

"And your last name?" she prompted.

"Gullible as hell," Noah murmured as he pulled back onto the road. "Just call me gullible as hell."

Chapter Two

"You need to eat."

Noah's comment penetrated Olivia's nervous preoccupation with the other diners in the small restaurant where they had stopped for lunch.

"Eat," he instructed, as he had done periodically since the waitress had placed the meat loaf-and-three-vegetable special in front of her.

Olivia knew she should be hungry enough to clean her plate, but who could think about food when at any moment a car of "suits" could drive up. She hadn't wanted to stop at all, but Noah had insisted.

She shot a nervous glance outside, where Puddin' waited in a truck cab cooled by a lowered window. Noah had also insisted the diner wouldn't welcome a dog, even a small one. Olivia wanted to wait in the truck with her pet, but Noah would have none of that, either. She was discovering her driver/rescuer was one bossy individual.

"How y'all doin'?" The hippy, flirtatious waitress sidled up to their table, as she had done at least a half dozen times. Her black-lacquered eyelashes fluttered in Noah's direction.

He grinned and held out his coffee cup. "Sure could use a refill."

She obliged with a simper that set Olivia's teeth on edge.

"You through, honey?" The waitress nodded at Olivia's plate.

"She's still working on it," Noah replied in his irritatingly superior tone.

She set her fork down. "Actually, I am finished."

Without asking, Noah ordered two pieces of coconut cream pie. Olivia protested. He offered her a quelling glance.

The waitress tittered and retreated, ample backside swaying in her pink gingham uniform.

Olivia sighed her frustration. "We really shouldn't leave Puddin' out there like this."

"The dog is fine. I'm not in the business of cruelty to animals."

"But still—"

"A person of limited means ought not to waste a free meal."

"I can pay for my own food," Olivia protested.

Noah looked skeptical as he lifted his mug. "Better save your money for later, when no one might be offering to feed you." He savored a long sip of coffee. "Just out of curiosity, how much money do you have?"

"Enough," was Olivia's evasive reply. In the two hours since he had agreed to take her to a bus station, Noah had done his best to dig information out of her. Where was she going? Did she have relatives she could call? How was she going to support herself? Of course, Olivia had told him nothing. Besides resenting his authoritative, prying manner, she didn't know the answer.

She had a vague notion about heading for Chicago. Just after college, she had spent part of one summer in a program at Chicago's Art Institute. A "suit" had been enrolled in the class, as well, to watch over her at all times, but still she had managed to enjoy the experience. She had made some contacts that summer that her father might not think to check right away. Maybe one of those acquaintances could help her land a job. Teaching perhaps. Working with children. She planned to take whatever job she could find. She had a first-class education. Surely that would count for something.

It had better. She had exactly $448.92 in her pocket, money scrounged from various handbags in her closet. A pair of diamond stud earrings and an opal ring were also in her tote bag.

She had left her engagement ring on her nightstand,

and the rest of her jewelry had been locked in a safe. She didn't feel right about taking any of it. She had left her credit cards behind, as well, not only because cash transactions would be harder to trace, but because she needed to do this on her own. She hoped the cash would get her on a bus and pay for a few days of expenses before she had to sell the jewelry. She wasn't going straight to Chicago, because that would be too easy to trace. She thought she would head northwest, then south, then to the east.

The waitress brought their pie, and to keep Noah off her back, Olivia downed her slice quickly. He, on the other hand, took his own sweet time.

"I could go for another slice," he said at last.

That was all Olivia could take. She scrambled out of the booth despite his protests. "I'll see you in the truck."

She stopped off in the rest room and frowned at her reflection in the mirror. The braids and absence of makeup made her look like a kid, an image enhanced by the rumpled T-shirt and jeans. Maybe her childish appearance was the reason Noah spoke to her as if she was a ninny. But the disguise might help her, as well. If anyone showed her photograph around this diner, surely the pigtailed ragamuffin she appeared to be wouldn't be associated with the well-dressed and coiffed Olivia Franklin.

A glance at her watch showed ten past noon. By now, she imagined the ranch was in a full-scale panic. It being her wedding day, she was certain no one would have been surprised when she didn't appear early in the morning. It had probably been at least ten—over three hours after Noah's truck had left the ranch—before Mary went to her room and found her gone.

Hopefully her father and the ''suits'' had latched on to the false trail she had attempted to leave—the reservation she had made on an early-morning flight out of Austin. The address book opened to an acquaintance from school who now lived in Madrid.

None of that would fool them for long. But surely they would chase those leads and talk to the caterers, who had not left the premises until the early hours of the morning. If she was lucky it would be a while before they considered Noah as the means of her escape.

By the time they launched a search for him, she hoped he would be on his way to Tennessee and she would be bound for Chicago by the most circuitous route possible. Which meant she needed to get on a bus—quickly.

This diner was a bus stop, but the next bus due in was only heading for the terminal in the county seat, which the waitress said was just twenty miles up the road. Olivia had pushed for Noah to keep going. But he had suggested…no, he had *insisted* they eat first, before he drove her on to the terminal.

After one last grimace at her reflection, Olivia settled her baseball cap on her head, pulled open the door and found herself face-to-face with a Texas state trooper.

Terror rooted her to the spot. Dear God, how could they have found her so soon?

"S'cuse me." The female officer stood back to allow Olivia to pass. The woman smiled, appearing altogether normal, as her polished brass buttons and badge gleamed.

Olivia forced her feet to move and kept her eyes turned downward as she slipped around the officer and into the diner's small vestibule. When she looked up, fear clutched at her stomach. Another trooper and two other uniformed lawmen were chatting with the hostess while waiting for a table to be cleared.

Not running out of the restaurant took all of Olivia's restraint. She pushed open the door, trying to appear casual and unconcerned before jogging across the parking lot toward the truck.

Puddin' greeted her with a friendly bark and jumped into her arms when the passenger door opened. "Get back inside," Olivia instructed. "Don't let anyone see you."

Instead, the dog leaped free and bounded around the truck, barking up a storm while Olivia gave chase. On the other side of the trailer they both came to a halt as a sheriff's patrol car slipped into a nearby parking space. Olivia fought the urge to scream.

Didn't these police officers have anything more important to do than hang out here eating pie?

Not even acknowledging this officer's presence,

she simply snatched Puddin' up and stalked back around the trailer. "I should have left you home, you rowdy mutt. You're going to ruin everything for both of us."

Noah, who was walking toward her, gave her an odd look as she climbed in the cab. He paused. "Everything all right?"

She nodded, watching the sheriff's deputy enter the diner. "I'm ready to go."

"I'm going to let the horse stretch her legs a bit."

"Here?" The word came out as a shriek.

Noah regarded her with narrowed blue eyes. "What's wrong with here?"

Casting nervous glances toward the diner where five officers where now ensconced, she scrambled for a reason. "I doubt that they want horse poop in the parking lot."

He gave a disgusted snort. "Like I would do something like that." He pulled the door open. "Get out. You can help me."

"Me?"

"Surely you know something about scraping up horse poop."

She wished she could tell him where to stick his horse poop and his domineering manner. But he had helped her. And she still needed him.

So she left Puddin' in the truck and followed Noah, thankful at least to have the trailer between herself and the diner's windows.

Seeing Royal Pleasure again was a joy, of course.

The horse nickered and nuzzled Olivia with her velvety nose.

"You work with her at Franklin's place?" Noah asked as they walked the horse through the parking lot. Away from the diner, thank God.

Trying desperately not to keep looking toward the diner, Olivia nodded. "Pleasure's the sweetest horse."

"And she breeds champions."

"Which is why you bought her."

"She belongs on my farm."

"Belongs?" Olivia shot him a quizzical look. "Why?"

He shrugged, his handsome features hardening. "Long story."

Olivia didn't push, though she studied her companion thoughtfully. Because her father had been dealing in horses for as long as she could remember, she had met plenty of breeders. Noah Raybourne looked more like a wrangler than the owner of a farm.

He was young. Probably in his early thirties. Tall and well built, he had the kind of shoulders that come from continuous hard work. His light-brown hair needed a trim, curling over his forehead and the collar of his worn denim shirt. His jaw was clean-shaven and square, and along with his generous mouth and nose, made for a strong profile. His face was altogether and emphatically male. Except for the long, dark lashes fringing his blue eyes. He wore his clothes with the casual unconcern of a working man. He hardly looked affluent enough to have purchased an animal like Royal Pleasure.

Curiosity getting the better of her, Olivia asked, "This farm you're talking about. It's really yours?"

"My grandfather started it. My father worked it. Now it's mine."

"Your father's retired?"

"He died." The terse answer invited no further comment from Olivia.

Noah walked Royal Pleasure a couple of times around the parking lot. And to Olivia's relief he merely asked her to lead the mare back to the trailer while he used a shovel and bucket to clean up after the horse.

Finally he flashed a grin at her as he walked Royal Pleasure up into the trailer. "I had you worried about that poop, didn't I?"

"Not at all."

"Yeah, you were worried." Still grinning, he stored the bucket and shovel, secured the horse and ramp and closed up the trailer. "I bet you've never shoveled anything in your life."

"Of course I have." Shoulders squaring, she started back to the truck. "Let's just get out of here."

Back in the driver's seat, Noah hesitated while Libby settled herself and her dog. Then he took firm hold of her hand, turning it palm side up. "This hand has never shoveled anything, much less horse sh— poop."

She snatched her fingers away. "That's not true."

He waited a moment, studying her small, set features. No one could doubt the determination in her jaw. Just as anyone could see she was completely freaked out about the police officers in the diner. In fact, she had been ready to jump right out of her skin the entire time they were eating. She almost ran out the door. Hell, she almost knocked him down trying to take the side of the booth facing the door.

"I have no doubt you are running from something," he said at last. "I just hope whatever it is doesn't land me in a passel of trouble, too."

She bit her lip. If her father figured out she was with Noah, who knew what sort of fuss he would make.

"Why don't you just tell me the truth?"

She remained silent, stroking her dog's fur and staring out the window.

"I might be able to help."

"You are helping. You're taking me to that bus station. That's all I need."

Noah let out a long sigh. "All right. I guess since we've come this far, I don't really need to know the truth."

Frowning, he navigated his rig out onto the highway. God only knew why he was compelled to know what she was hiding. Or why he felt so sorry for her. More of that sense of honor he had learned from his mother, probably. The same inclinations had led him to rescue injured squirrels, champion the nerdiest kids at school and stand up to his no-account stepfather.

Nine times out of ten his good intentions had ended up costing him. Why couldn't he learn?

With his luck, Libby was duping him but good, playing on his sympathies with her big, brown eyes, her cute behind, her tears and that bruise on her arm. He wished to hell he didn't feel this compunction to rescue her.

They drove for quite a distance in silence, while Noah darted glances at her pale face. She kept leaning forward, studying the mirror on the passenger's side.

"You think one of those officers might come after us?" he asked.

She said nothing, but the frantic glance she sent toward the mirror spoke volumes.

"Just tell me this much. Is Roger Franklin going to be really angry with me?"

"Would you please be quiet?" she demanded. "You're making me nervous."

"Because I'm close to the truth. You've got something that Roger Franklin's going to want back, haven't you?"

"No!"

"Quit lying. What is it? Did you hide it somewhere in the camper?"

"No."

"In your bag, maybe?"

"Please just shut up!"

"Don't I have a right to know what I've helped you steal from Roger Franklin?"

"I didn't steal anything," she exclaimed. "It's me

he'll be looking for.'' The words seemed to burst out of her. "I'm what he'll want.''

"What are you saying?''

She twisted around to face him, the dog whining on her lap. "Roger Franklin is my father. I'm running away from him.''

Dread kicked Noah in the belly like a fist.

Roger Franklin's daughter. Good God, the man was going to kill him.

Later, Noah wasn't sure how he got the truck off the highway. All he remembered was turning into the parking lot of what appeared to be an abandoned produce stand.

Moments after coming to a stop, he dragged Libby—*yeah, like that was her name*—and her dog across the front seat and outside the driver's side door.

Once her feet touched the ground, she jerked away from him. "You don't have to manhandle me.''

"I ought to do worse than that!'' Noah let loose the crudest, most vulgar curses he could think of while he paced back and forth in front of her.

Libby huddled against the truck, clutching Puddin'.

Noah turned and stopped. "Are you saying Roger Franklin bruised your arm?''

Her answer was a slow, miserable shake of her head. "I fell out of a window while I was escaping.'' She had the grace to at least look ashamed of having misled him about the bruise.

"You went *out the window? Ran away?*" Noah was just beginning to comprehend her choice of words. "Wait a minute. How old are you?"

She swallowed hard. "Almost twenty-four."

He cursed again. "You're an adult. Why couldn't you just leave through the front door?"

"It's complicated."

"Tell me."

Her sigh was dramatic. "Can't you just take me on to the bus?"

"No!" he shouted. "From the looks of the security around your home, I don't think your father takes kindly to anyone making off with what's his. And he just might think I took you. So you owe me some kind of explanation."

"You're not going to understand—"

"Try me," he ordered.

And so her tale unfolded. Her mother's kidnapping and murder. Her father's fears and overprotectiveness. Olivia's many tries at freedom. Her plans to marry Marshall Crane. Her realization that marriage would only trap her further.

Only then did Noah break in. "You mean you're the daughter who was supposed to get married today?"

"I'm the only daughter."

Blood pounded in his temples. "And you just took off."

"I told you. I couldn't marry Marshall."

"And what about him? Did you bother telling him you were leaving?"

"He would have stopped me."

"Don't you think you owed him some kind of explanation?"

"It's not as if Marshall loved me or anything."

"Then why marry you?"

She managed a short laugh. "I already told you. Marrying me was a way to cement his place in my father's company."

"He must have cared about you."

"I'm sure he cared," was her impatient, offhand reply. "But it wasn't about love. I don't see what this has to do—"

"Right about now this Marshall guy is probably realizing he got stood up. On his wedding day. At the altar."

"I doubt he'll even go to the church."

"And does that somehow make it better?"

She took a step to the side, edging away from him. "I don't see why you're so concerned about Marshall."

Noah pushed his face down close to hers. "Libby, or whatever your name is—"

"Olivia," she supplied.

"I'm concerned about Marshall because I know how he feels. I've been in his place. Standing there. Waiting for a bride who doesn't show."

Understanding dawned slowly in her expression. "I'm sorry, but that's still—"

"You should have had the decency to tell him."

"And then I wouldn't have gotten away."

"You haven't gotten away." Stepping in front of her, Noah bracketed her slender body with both his arms, pinning her and her dog to the truck. "We're going back."

"I can't."

"You don't have a choice."

She pushed against his chest, anger sparking in her gaze while the dog whimpered a protest. "I know you've done me a favor, but you're not the boss of me—"

"You made me the boss by sneaking into my rig."

"But—"

"And lying to me." Noah gripped her shoulders, leaning in even closer. He could smell the faint trace of her expensive perfume, could see the light sprinkling of freckles across her upturned nose. She looked so damned innocent, so sweet and vulnerable. He could be fooled by her. Fooled very easily.

As if she sensed him wavering, the big, doe eyes she'd fastened on him filled with tears. "I'm sorry I lied to you. Really I am. I just had to get away. I was desperate. Haven't you ever been desperate?"

What he knew about desperation she couldn't begin to imagine, Noah thought. He understood all too well feeling trapped and frightened. Compared to him, this woman didn't know the meaning of the word.

Returning fury thickened his voice. "What the hell were you thinking, using me this way?"

"I had to get away."

"Didn't you think your father might assume you went with me? Or that I took you? With your father so worried about you being snatched, isn't it logical that I might be a kidnapping suspect?"

The muscles in her throat worked as she swallowed. "I never thought about that."

"Poor little rich girls like you never think about other people, do you?"

Color suffused her cheeks. "That's not fair. I'm not like that."

He had to laugh. "So now I'm supposed to think you're spoiled but good-hearted."

"I am not spoiled."

Her protest barely registered with Noah as he warmed to his subject. "You're spoiled and weak and heartless. Anyone with a heart wouldn't just leave their groom without an explanation."

"But you don't see—"

"I see all right," he muttered. "I see a pathetic *woman* acting like a child. If you wanted out of your father's house, all you had to do was go through the door."

"It wasn't that simple."

"He chained you up? Beat you?" Noah glanced down at the dog she clutched like a lifeline. "Did he threaten to kill your dog if you tried to leave?"

She blanched. "Of course not. He's not a monster."

"Then why all this drama? Sneaking out. Stowing

away with me." Noah regarded her with disgust. "It sounds to me like you're just a little child who likes to play games and create big dramas so Daddy will come racing in."

"You couldn't be more off-base."

"Just do everyone a favor and get some therapy to deal with your daddy complex."

Olivia had never in her life wanted to hit anyone like she wanted to punch this big, sanctimonious man. She settled for grinding her foot into his.

Shouting a curse, he released his grip on her, and she ducked away. She'd be damned if she would stand here and let him pronounce judgments on her actions. He didn't know her life, didn't understand the forces at work between her and her father.

Noah clearly had other ideas. He hobbled around the truck and stopped her just as she was dragging her bag from the passenger seat. "Where do you think you're going?"

"I'm absolving you of any part in my 'little game,'" she retorted. "Thank you and goodbye."

"Too late for that. What'll I say when the police or your father's private security force track me down and haul me in for questioning?"

"I don't care."

"And if they decide to throw me in the pokey?"

She made an impatient sound and stalked around the front of the truck. "Now who's creating a drama?"

He took hold of her arm again. "Just shut up and get in the truck."

"No!" She jerked her arm from his grip. "I'm not going back. If you try to force me, then you really will be in trouble."

"Get in the damn truck." Without waiting to see if she would comply, he swooped in and picked her up.

Olivia was too busy hanging on to a hysterically yapping Puddin' to fight Noah very hard. She cursed him instead, calling on each and every one of the limited number of obscenities she knew. Then she repeated them again.

He was trying to maneuver her and the dog toward the passenger door when a patrol car sped by on the road.

"Oh, hell," Noah muttered as the car slowed.

The car turned down a road to the right.

"Maybe they didn't see us," Olivia murmured.

"Yeah, right," Noah agreed sarcastically. "This big, white horse trailer is hard to miss. Especially with the two of us in hand-to-hand combat here on the side of the road."

"But they might not even be looking for us."

The words were no sooner out of her mouth when the sound of sirens split the air.

The next few moments unfolded like a slow-motion scene in a movie. Three police vehicles—state patrol and sheriff's—descended one after the other, brakes screeching, raising clouds of dust and gravel. The female officer from the diner was the first to bail out of her vehicle and crouch behind her open car door, calling for Noah to put Olivia down.

Dazed, Olivia said, "They've got guns."

A white line around his mouth, Noah glared at her. Then she landed in a sputtering heap in the dust.

Noah stepped over her and advanced, hands held high, toward the officers, calling out, "She's Roger Franklin's daughter, but I'm not a kidnapper. Just take her away. I beg of you, take her away."

Chapter Three

The sheriff's office was located in the county court-house, right on the central square of the town where Noah and Olivia had been headed. From the small, barred window of the holding room where she and Puddin' waited, Olivia could see the bus station sign. She had been so close to freedom.

If only they hadn't stopped for lunch.

Apparently news of her disappearance had gone out from her father's ranch to the police in the eastern counties of Texas just after she and Noah left the diner. One sheriff's deputy remembered Olivia with Puddin'. All the officers, who had been meeting for a regular weekly lunch, remembered the horse trailer. So they had started after Noah and Olivia. One car spotted them and called for backup.

"Then everyone descended like gung-ho storm troopers," Olivia had told the sheriff with no small amount of outrage. "It was simply ridiculous. They treated Noah like a criminal."

The sheriff's sunburned brow had wrinkled in consternation. "I'm sorry, Miss Franklin, but at that time, we had reason to think he might be a criminal."

"Oh, baloney," she had retorted. "If I had been kidnapped, don't you think I might have told the trooper who was in the bathroom with me at the diner?"

"People who are in fear for their lives can exhibit some mighty unusual behavior," the sheriff explained. "Sometimes they don't ask for help."

Olivia would have none of that, either. "In the first place, isn't it more than a little unusual for a kidnapper to stop at a diner with his captive? And then stick around to walk his horse with five officers chowing down nearby?"

Unable to explain away that part of the scenario, the sheriff had flushed an even darker shade of red and excused himself.

This conversation had taken place just after Olivia and Puddin' had been placed in this room. A move that had followed a screaming and barking marathon precipitated by the sight of Noah being led into the office in handcuffs.

Olivia whispered to Puddin', "Those handcuffs were the stupidest move yet." The dog yapped her agreement.

In the hour since the sheriff had interviewed Olivia and left her alone with an underling at guard by the door, she had imagined Noah in another part of the office being manhandled by big, bubba officers who were determined to get at the truth of her so-called kidnapping.

If Noah had been harmed in any way, she was going to make sure he received a handsome settlement. In fact, he deserved something even if he had not been harmed. As domineering and pushy as he had been, he had also tried to help her. She had repaid him by getting him in trouble, just as he had said she would. Maybe she really was the spoiled, thoughtless little child he had accused her of being.

She flushed with shame. Maybe it was time she faced some hard truths about herself.

She still couldn't believe her father had reported her kidnapped. It spoke to his money and influence that he had been able to convince the authorities to put out such a bulletin. There had been no sign of struggle at their home. No ransom demand. Nothing but her father's paranoia and his ability to wield his power.

A knock on the door sent Puddin' scurrying under a chair and snapped Olivia out of her reverie. The guard poked his head in. "Your father's coming, Miss Franklin. He *coptered* in from Austin." The young officer looked so impressed with this news that Olivia wanted to smack him.

After he closed the door, she began counting down

the minutes until the storm would hit the building. She was nearing seven when she heard the shouting in the hall. Puddin' barked and jumped into Olivia's lap. Then the door slammed open, and her father strode in, his face a thundercloud. In the hall outside, Olivia glimpsed two of the "suits."

"Dear Lord in Heaven," her father said, crossing the small space to where she sat, elbows propped on a scarred wooden table. "Why have they got you locked in like this?"

"Probably because I threatened to punch one of the officers in the nose."

Roger Franklin's normally florid complexion paled. "Now why did you do that?"

"Because this whole thing is a stupid mess. There was no reason, absolutely no reason at all, for me or Noah Raybourne to be hauled in like common criminals."

"I thought Raybourne had taken you."

"That's crap and you know it."

Her father went stiff with shock. Olivia had never spoken to him like this in her life. Even when she had been pushing hardest for independence, she had reserved her shouting and tears for later, when she was alone in her room or with Mary to comfort her. But she was tired of the civility that had netted her a big, fat zero. Maybe it was time to change.

She pushed back her chair and stood with her dog in her arms. "I want you to get Noah and that sheriff in here."

Her father's face darkened. "Now you just listen here, Olivia Kay—"

"I'm not talking to you unless they're in here!" Olivia shouted. Puddin' growled.

Roger glared at Olivia for what felt like a full minute, obviously expecting her to back down. She stood her ground. He made an impatient gesture to the "suits," who disappeared.

A moment or two ticked past in silence while her father took a seat at the table and studied her through narrowed eyes. "I don't know what in the world has gotten into you."

"Don't you think it's about time I grew up?"

"This isn't grown-up," he shot back. "Running off like this on your wedding day is the mark of immaturity and recklessness, the sort of behavior I thought you were through with a long time ago."

"Would you listen to yourself? You talk to me as if I'm twelve years old."

"If that's the way you act…"

Puddin' gave a welcoming bark, and Olivia looked up to see Noah standing in the doorway, the sheriff behind him.

She took a step toward Noah. "I am so sorry about all this."

Her father got up and came toward Noah, as well. "Yes, Raybourne, I apologize, too. I'm sorry my daughter's foolish escapade resulted in this mess. I don't know why she acted so stupidly."

Olivia flushed crimson at her father's words, feeling like a disobedient child caught with her hand in the cookie jar.

Noah started to say something but was cut off when the sheriff pushed past him and into the room. "All right, now. Everyone just settle down." He scowled at the two "suits" who crowded in behind Noah. "You two, you get out of here."

"My men—" Roger began.

"Can wait outside," the sheriff said with quiet force. After the "suits" reluctantly obeyed, he gestured for Noah to take a seat along the wall, opposite the table where Roger Franklin sat and Olivia stood.

The officer ran a hand through his thinning hair and sent a frown around the room. "From what I can determine, this is a family matter that had been blown up all out of proportion." He nodded at Noah. "Mr. Raybourne, you are free to go, with our apologies for any inconvenience."

Noah got to his feet. "That's all right, Sheriff. I understand you were just trying to do your job. Something that's not always easy when rich, spoiled brats are involved."

The contempt in his gaze caused a peculiar stab of pain in Olivia's chest. "I am really so sorry," she said again. "I know those words are inadequate for what you've gone through today. Dealing with me. Facing down a bunch of overexcited police officers. Getting dragged in here in handcuffs. Nothing I can say can make up for all that, but I hope you realize I am truly, truly sorry."

Noah did not reply, but Olivia thought she detected a softening in his expression. She wasn't sure why it felt so important for him not to hate her.

Roger cleared his throat impatiently and withdrew his checkbook. "I want to show you my gratitude, Raybourne."

"That's not necessary," Noah retorted, his jaw squaring.

"But I insist." Roger took out a pen and filled out the check with a flourish. "Raybourne, I'm sure your little operation will benefit from this."

Noah went still at the word "little." Olivia wasn't really surprised when he shook his head at the check her father proffered.

"I can't take it," Noah said. "I don't expect to be paid for helping out someone in trouble."

"Yes, but Olivia wasn't really in trouble," Roger replied, still holding out the check. "She was simply being a brat, as you said."

Noah sent Olivia a look that she couldn't quite decipher. "She was pretty desperate to get away."

Roger laid the check on the table and recapped his pen. "She didn't really want to get away. She was just overwhelmed by the wedding."

"I didn't want the wedding," Olivia said.

Her father shot a long-suffering smile toward the sheriff. "You don't mean that."

Anger thickened Olivia's voice. "I'm sick and tired of being told what I want, what I should do and think and feel. It's way past time that I started thinking and acting on my own. I should be on my own.''

Her father rolled his eyes. ''Nonsense. You wouldn't know the first thing to do on your own.'' His gaze swept over her. ''You couldn't take care of that dog of yours. Much less yourself.''

His dismissive cruelty, displayed so callously in front of strangers, momentarily robbed Olivia of speech. All these years she had told herself he was overprotective because he loved her so much. When had the desire to keep her safe changed to a complete disregard for her abilities? For some reason he thought she didn't have the brains or the wits to take care of herself.

''What's wrong with you?'' she demanded when she found her voice would work again. ''Did what happened to Mother warp you to the point that you can't see me as a real, live human being? When did I become just one more possession to you?''

''You're being hysterical.'' Roger rose and held out his hand. ''Come along now. We'll go home, and you can talk to Marshall—''

''I do owe Marshall an apology,'' Olivia said, glancing at Noah. ''It was cowardly of me to run away instead of going to him and explaining why I couldn't marry him.''

''Yes, it was cowardly,'' Roger agreed, extending his hand again. ''Marshall's waiting at the ranch. I feel sure he'll forgive you. The wedding can be re-scheduled.''

"No, it can't."

"Olivia—"

"Can't you hear me at all?" Olivia demanded of her father.

"I simply don't listen when you're acting like a fool."

Reeling as if she had been punched, Olivia faced the sheriff. "Am I free to go?"

"Certainly. Anytime your father—"

"I don't care about my father," Olivia cut in. "I'm not going anywhere with him."

Roger sputtered a protest, which Olivia ignored. She gathered up her tote bag and started for the door, pausing only in front of Noah. "Thank you for everything. You were absolutely right. I really didn't need this drama to walk out, did I? I should have just done it long ago."

Noah wasn't certain why he was so impressed with Olivia. Was she playing a new game, pretending she was leaving, so that her father would give chase again? There was something about the calm in her voice and the determination in her expression that told him she was serious. After witnessing this little scene with her father, he hoped she was getting away. No one deserved to be belittled and talked to as her father had talked to her.

"Olivia, come back here," Roger Franklin demanded as she opened the door.

Franklin's men stepped in front of her, closing her

escape route. She turned to the sheriff again. "Is there any reason why I have to do what my father wants?"

The officer shot Franklin a nervous glance. Noah couldn't say he blamed the man for worrying about getting on the bad side of one of the richest men in Texas. But the truth was the truth. The sheriff cleared his throat. "Miss Franklin, there's no legal reason why you have to stay here or go with your father."

"You cannot do this," her father insisted, panic clearly breaking through his calm facade. "You're too inexperienced and naive to make it a day by yourself. What are you going to do for money?"

"I'll get a job."

"Doing what?"

"That's none of your concern," Olivia retorted proudly. With that, she pushed past the burly guards, who gave way with obvious reluctance. Noah felt a definite spark of admiration and something like pride.

"Olivia," her father called angrily, going to the door. "You keep walking, and you're on your own. I won't rescue you. Do you hear me? I'm done with you if you walk out the door."

Olivia didn't reappear, much to Noah's relief.

Her father ordered his men to follow her.

Noah could no longer contain his thoughts. "Good God, Franklin, why can't you just let her go?"

"You don't understand what could happen to her."

"I understand you're some kind of warped control freak." Noah shook his head in disgust. "Olivia tried to explain to me why she couldn't just walk out, free and clear, like any normal adult. Now I see exactly what she was talking about.''

''You don't see anything,'' Franklin replied. ''Olivia belongs at home, where she's safe.''

''She belongs wherever the hell she wants to be.'' Noah turned to the sheriff. ''Can your men make sure Franklin's two goons don't bother her?''

With smug satisfaction, the sheriff said, ''It will be my pleasure.'' He left the room without a backward glance.

Franklin blew out a frustrated breath. ''Raybourne, I can see you managed to put some real ideas in Olivia's mind during your few, short hours together.''

''I put ideas in her head?'' Noah shook his head. ''It wasn't me who told her to climb out a window and stow away in my camper like some runaway slave. She was determined to get away from you before I ever entered the picture.''

The other man gave him a considering glance. ''It occurs to me that a young, ambitious man like yourself might have thought about the advantages of becoming involved with a rich young woman like my daughter.''

Noah did a slow burn. ''I can assure you that becoming involved with your daughter is the least desirable thing I can think of. I went that route once, and I'm not interested in taking it again.''

A few moments passed while Franklin continued to study Noah. ''You know, I believe you,'' he said at last. Noah could almost see the wheels turning in the man's brain. "I think you're exactly what you seem, Raybourne. A truly honest and aboveboard man."

Deciding he'd had enough of this blowhard, Noah headed for the door. "I have a terrible feeling you're buttering me up for some reason, Mr. Franklin. Whatever you're going to ask me, the answer is no. I've got a horse I need to get to my farm. Unlike you, I'm a working man who can't afford to waste any more time."

"I'm sure there are a great many things you can't afford."

The drawled comment made Noah's hands fist at his sides. "Good day, Franklin."

"If you did me a favor, I could tear up that check you wrote me for Royal Pleasure. I could give you the horse."

Noah knew he would be better off to just keep walking. He should get in his truck, drive away and be done with the Franklins—father and daughter— once and for all. But the memory of the check he had written last night was very clear. That money represented all of his savings, definitely more than he could afford to spend. If he had that money *and* Royal Pleasure. The mere thought made him hesitate.

Franklin added, "I'll sweeten the deal. You can have the check I just wrote, as well."

He was referring to the check he had written just a little while ago, the check Noah had refused without even knowing the amount.

"It's five thousand dollars," the older man said. "That should pay for a whole lot of feed and supplies for your farm. Help me out and there might even be five thousand more in the deal."

Noah wanted to resist, but he was only human. He turned around and looked Franklin in the eye. "What do you want?"

"My daughter needs looking after."

"I'm not a baby-sitter."

"Give her a job on your farm. She knows horses. Put her to work. I'll give you the money to pay her a salary."

Remembering Olivia's distress over the thought of shoveling horse piles, Noah had to laugh. "Forgive me if I can't imagine your little princess working with her hands."

Again Franklin seemed to lose himself in thought. Finally he said, "Maybe it would do her good."

For the first time Noah saw a glimmer of real emotion in the man's expression.

"Olivia's right to say I've protected her," Franklin continued. "Maybe I was wrong to think keeping her from the real world was what was best. Maybe it is true that I've made her afraid. That might be why I've come to not like her very much."

Hearing a father admit he didn't like his child aroused real pity in Noah. "Protecting her is one thing. Treating her like she's an idiot is another. Olivia is no dummy, even though you seem to want to treat her that way."

The older man nodded, a contemplative look on his face. "I'd like you to look after her this summer. I don't mean give her a cushy vacation. Be hard on her. Show her how tough it can be out there."

"You think that will have her running home in double time, don't you?"

"Either that or she'll be able to stand on her own two feet."

Noah was left to wonder which outcome Roger Franklin wanted more.

Pensiveness gone, the man turned all business once again. "How about it, Raybourne? Do we have a deal?"

This was wrong, a tiny voice inside Noah whispered. The same code of ethics that stopped him from leaving Olivia alone on the road told him this wasn't right. If he took this money and gave her a job, he would be deceiving her.

But what was she going to do if he didn't help her? She had walked out of here determined to make it on her own, though she didn't have a clue about what that entailed. She was full of determination, but that hadn't disguised the vulnerability lurking just beneath the surface. Someone might very well take advantage of her.

Still ignoring the proffered check, Noah asked Franklin, "What makes you think she'll go anywhere with me?"

"She'll go," her father replied. "No matter what Olivia says, she's frightened right now. She doesn't know where she's going or how she's going to support herself.''

Noah nodded his agreement. He knew Olivia hadn't thought much beyond getting away from her father. But she was right to be trying to escape. Franklin was clearly selfish and manipulative. If Noah didn't help Olivia, her father might pursue her until she gave in and went back. Maybe Noah could help her get away once and for all. He wasn't certain why he felt duty-bound to help her, but he did.

Franklin continued, ''She'll gladly accept a job from you. If she stays and works out the summer, you get the horse and the extra money.'' He held out the check to Noah again. ''Do we have a deal or not?''

The zeros at the end of the five were tempting. Noah tried not to be swayed by the knowledge that this money and saving the cost of Royal Pleasure could push his struggling breeding operation into the black.

As if reading his mind, Franklin said, ''Just think of this as a business deal, Raybourne. You'll be performing a service for me. This is payment.''

But I'll really be performing a service for Olivia, Noah told himself. *And if I take the check, I can help myself and her, at the same time.*

Only half-satisfied with that rationalization, Noah accepted the money.

Franklin smiled. ''Come on. My men can tell us where Olivia has taken herself off to.''

* * *

Who knew dogs weren't allowed on buses?

With a ragged sigh of weariness, Olivia planted herself on a bench outside the front door of the Greyhound Bus Station. Beside her, Puddin' looked up with ever-hopeful, bright eyes. "You're a lot of trouble," Olivia told her pet.

In response, the dog nuzzled her with her cold, wet nose, and Olivia hugged her. From her tote, she retrieved a small bag of kibble and offered some to the grateful pet. Yes, the companionship was well worth all the trouble. It looked as if Puddin' was all Olivia had in the world.

Minutes ticked past while the late-afternoon sun slanted across the lazy activity of this small, Texas town. Olivia knew she should be taking some sort of action, but she wasn't sure what it was going to be. She didn't have enough money to buy a car, no credit card for renting one. The bus was out. There were no planes or passenger trains. Perhaps she could call one of her few friends from college to ask for help, but she honestly hated the thought.

Once or twice she directed a quick glance up the street, half expecting to see her father striding down the sidewalk from the courthouse. There was no one on the sidewalk at all. The "suits" who had trailed her from the courthouse were gone, warned away by the sheriff and one of his deputies. The sheriff had kindly inquired if he could be of any assistance to her. She had declined, and he had left her alone to try and buy a bus ticket.

So here she was. On her own. Free at last. Why wasn't she ecstatic?

Maybe because she was afraid her father was right. Maybe she was too inexperienced and naive to survive on her own. A lump rose in her throat when she remembered the way he had treated her. Even though she knew he didn't think much of her, it had hurt like hell for him to berate her in front of everyone. Especially in front of Noah.

Another glance up the street confirmed that Noah's truck and trailer were truly gone. No doubt he had raced out of town as soon as he could. Probably while she was inside the bus station, begging the ticket agent to allow Puddin' on the bus. The woman, who sported a beehive hairdo and rhinestone-studded glasses, had been downright nasty. She had even taken exception to Puddin' visiting the bathroom with Olivia.

"Maybe I can hide you in my tote bag," Olivia said to Puddin'.

The dog barked in reply, then jumped from the bench and danced across the sidewalk on two hind legs.

"What in the world's the matter with you?" Olivia found the answer to her question in the truck and trailer that were pulling into the parking spaces in front of the bench. Puddin' barked as if greeting an old friend.

Olivia tried very hard not to be just as happy to see Noah as he leaned out of his opened window. In fact, she stretched her dusty, jeans-clad legs out in front of her and pretended elaborate disinterest.

"Bought a ticket yet?" Noah asked.

She lifted her chin and lied, "Yes, we're waiting here for the bus."

"I thought the buses pulled in around back."

"It's nicer sitting here."

A line appeared between Noah's eyebrows. "Do you even have enough money for a ticket?"

The concern in his voice set Olivia's teeth on edge. Only an hour ago he had regarded her with contempt. She could do without his pity now. "Whether or not I have a dime is of no concern to you, Mr. Raybourne."

Noah scowled. "There's no need to cop an attitude with me. What happened to the person who was *so really, truly sorry* for all the trouble she caused me?"

"I'm still sorry," Olivia retorted. "I just fail to see why you're continuing to take an interest in me. I figured you'd be halfway out of town by now."

"Yeah...well..." He drummed his fingers on the side of his door. "It's just that I started thinking about you standing up to your father."

Avoiding his gaze, Olivia fiddled with the end of one braid. "I should have done that a long time ago."

"He's kind of jerk, your father."

"Yes," she agreed. "He is."

"But I don't figure you planned on him just washing his hands of you."

Anger flared inside her. "I know you think I staged this whole thing just so my father would chase me down. You're wrong. All I wanted was to get away. So now I have. I'm perfectly fine about everything, thank you very much."

Noah's expression was filled with disbelief, but he said nothing.

"Is there anything else you want?" Olivia demanded when he didn't move on after a few moments.

"I was thinking of offering you a job."

"What?"

"On my farm. Working with my horses."

She regarded him with suspicion. "What kind of joke are you pulling?"

"It's not a joke. I could see by the way you were with Royal Pleasure that you enjoy horses. I need some extra help around my place this summer. My mother…she runs this camp and well…I know you need a job. How about it?"

Olivia couldn't quite believe her ears. She stood, hands on her hips and advanced toward the truck. "Let me get this straight. You're interested in hiring a rich, little, spoiled brat?"

He ducked his head, looking positively shame-faced. "I'm sorry for calling you that. It's obvious you've had a lot to put up with from your father."

"And having gotten rid of him, I'm not interested

in going to work for you.'' She bent and picked up Puddin', retrieved her tote from the bench and started down the sidewalk, back toward the sheriff's office.

Behind her, Noah called her name. ''Where are you going? I thought you had a bus to catch.''

She kept walking, her shoulders held stubbornly straight.

''Come on, Olivia,'' he called out, easing the truck alongside her. ''I pulled in the back of the bus station, went in looking for you and found out you couldn't get a ticket with that mu—I mean, with Puddin'. I know you don't have anywhere to go.''

She turned and glared at him. ''Just go away.''

''Olivia…''

She wheeled to face him then. ''What do you want?''

''To help you?'' he offered.

''I can't imagine why.''

He wouldn't quite meet her eyes. ''I just think you need a break.''

''I can't imagine what's changed your tune about me, but I'm not interested in your charity.''

''I expect you to work, and I'm going to pay you. Maybe it'll give you time to think through what you want.''

Time. Now that was an appealing prospect. Just being someplace safe and comfortable but away from her father would be heavenly relief. She could call up her acquaintances in Chicago, get them looking around for some sort of job and save up the money

Noah would pay her. By the end of the summer she might have enough to make a real start.

Noah could see her wavering. He felt like a complete heel for playing on her insecurities this way. But, hell, he had already made his deal with the devil, what else could he do that was any more wrong? Maybe some good would come out of it. This little princess would learn what it was to do an honest day's work, and Raybourne Farms would gain Royal Pleasure without expending a dime.

"You really want me to work for you?" Olivia asked.

He wanted her to work for him like he wanted his finest stud to go sterile. But aside from the deal he had struck with her father, Noah had to consider what might happen if she walked away right now. The late-afternoon light played over her pale features, highlighting the dark circles under her eyes and the weariness around her mouth. She looked young and vulnerable. Just what was she going to do if she didn't come with him?

He set the brake on the truck, opened the door and got out to take Olivia's bag from her. "Come on," he said, as kindly as possible. "You're worn out, and I'd like to get a few miles down the road before we have to stop for the night. Let's go."

She hesitated only a moment more. "I still don't know why you're doing this. I'm not sure I should trust you."

Grunting in reply, he held the door open wide. She

took a deep breath, then scrambled across the seat, giving him an altogether pleasant view of her wriggling, curvy little butt.

He silently counted to ten and climbed in after her. He said nothing when her useless dog nestled against his leg instead of hers.

"It's okay," he assured Olivia, when she started to retrieve the mutt. "Anything's better than her yapping."

"She really likes you."

Wondering whether to feel blessed or cursed, Noah tried to ignore his passengers and concentrate on the road. According to his map, there was a campground not too far out of town. They could stay there tonight. The camper had two beds. After all they had been through today, surely Olivia wouldn't mind sharing....

That thought trailed away when Noah noticed Olivia had loosened her braids. Who would know those two thick ropes were hiding such glorious red-gold curls. She ran her fingers along her scalp, and gorgeous, full-bodied hair sprang to life, curling about her shoulders, gleaming in the fading sunlight.

The baseball-capped, pigtailed and moderately attractive young woman he had chased out of his camper and dropped in the dirt was transformed. The hair framed and softened her features. She looked...womanly. Desirable. Sexy as hell.

While Noah was trying to digest the spectacular changes, Olivia dug through her tote and finally retrieved a brush. "This stupid hair," she muttered as she hung her head forward and dragged the brush through the bottom layer. "It's so heavy and so hot. I'm going to cut it all—"

His protest was a strangled, half-garbled plea.

Olivia swung her head up, and a sweet, perfumed scent filled the truck's cab as her hair settled in layers about her shoulders. "Did you say something?" she asked, her brown eyes wide.

He cleared his throat. "We're going to stop at a motel tonight. I'll sleep in the camper. You'll take the room."

"But—"

"No arguments, okay?" Noah focused on the road, trying to ignore the growing tightness at his crotch.

"How long are we going to be on the road?" Olivia asked.

"At least two more days."

Two long days. Closed up in this truck with her. Dear Lord, what had he done?

Noah darted another glance at Olivia. At the curtain of red-gold silk that just begged for a man's touch. At her pouty rosebud of a mouth. At the breasts that filled her T-shirt with such soft, appealing fullness. Why hadn't he noticed any of this before?

"It's going to be a long trip," he murmured. "Real long."

Olivia made no reply. Noah squirmed in his seat, trying to get comfortable. That's when he noticed Puddin' squinting up at him. The dog looked almost…disapproving. As if she knew exactly what Noah had on his mind.

He cracked the window to let some air blow in his face. It wasn't quite the cold shower he needed, but it helped. God knew, he was going to need all the help he could get on this trip.

Chapter Four

For someone who had spent her entire life under wraps, the road from East Texas to Middle Tennessee was filled with incredible discoveries.

First, there was the discount store where Olivia purchased jeans and shirts, underwear and toiletries. She had never been in such a place and could have wandered the aisles for hours if Noah hadn't been waiting impatiently outside with her dog and his horse.

Then there was the roadside Arkansas barbecue stand where Noah stopped and bought their lunch. To Olivia, the pulled pork tasted as divine as the finest caviar. Better, actually.

The fireworks stands along the interstate exits puzzled her. So many of them, one right after the other, where sparklers were advertised at ninety-nine cents a package, and cherry bombs were a guaranteed big bang. How did anyone choose among products and deals that sounded exactly alike?

The Praise the Lord signs and attendant warnings of doom that decorated trees and utility poles astonished her. Sunday morning, she kept asking Noah to stop at one of the many small churches they passed. She wanted to know if the services would match the fiercely advertised assertions of a coming apocalypse and the promised escape for the righteous.

Noah wouldn't stop. Neither would he take her to visit an advertised rattlesnake ranch. Or Graceland in Memphis. Or Loretta Lynn's ranch outside of Nashville. He wouldn't hear of letting her out of the truck to aid in the rescue of hundreds of chicks who were escaping a wrecked eighteen-wheeler.

Noah, Olivia decided, was entirely too cautious. She told him, the next time she drove across the country, she was going alone. With a long-suffering glare, he offered to pay her way.

Before now, Olivia had seen life from behind the protective smoked glass of a limousine. When she had traveled with her father, she had seen only airports, hotel rooms and carefully selected tourist stops. Beaches, historic structures, resorts. A whole new world beckoned to her from beyond the cab of the truck, a world that seemed more colorful, more immediate and more alluring than anything she had ever seen before.

Olivia suspected Noah would have been content to pass their journey together in relative silence. But the knowledge that she was free of her father's boundaries made her too restless to watch the passing landscape, however fascinating, all the time. So she made him talk to her.

It wasn't really too difficult. All she had to do was find the right subject. Which, for Noah, was his farm.

He could go on for hours about his horses. Four prize-winning stallions were available for stud service. Five foals had arrived this spring, fewer than he had hoped when he bred his mares, but still a good number. He thought the three yearlings he was presently offering for sale would bring a good price.

According to Noah, there was simply no better breed than the Tennessee Walking Horse. Naturally gentle, their inherited gait was the famous running walk. Having ridden a number of Tennessee Walkers, including Royal Pleasure, Olivia was familiar with their smooth and easy ride. From Noah she got a quick education in the development of the breed, whose beginnings were just miles from the Middle Tennessee county where Raybourne Farms was located.

Noah spoke with complete and utter pride in his business. He said he was struggling, asserting that fact with a fierceness that almost dared her to comment. It was clear he had big, big dreams. He hinted that the farm had once been very successful, but any attempt by Olivia to delve into personal territory that might explain its downfall was met with a change of subject. The most personal information she managed to get out of him was that his mother lived in her own house on the farm.

Olivia envied Noah his passion. For all of his life he had planned and worked and dreamed of running his farm. A place his grandfather built, where his parents had lived, where his own children would someday work and play.

What would it be like to have such a dream? That question nibbled at Olivia's subconscious late on the afternoon of their third day on the road. For most of her life she had simply dreamed of being free. Now she was. And what was she going to do with her life? Olivia figured she had a whole summer ahead to settle on her dreams.

Outside her window, rain streamed over the skyscrapers of Nashville. She could feel Noah's rising excitement. Even Puddin' sat up, peering ahead, as if the farm would appear at any moment.

After about a forty-minute drive southeast from Nashville, they arrived. And it was far from the ramshackle operation Olivia expected.

Noah had forgotten to describe the long, gray stone fence that announced the entrance to the driveway. Nor had he mentioned the tall, ancient trees that bordered that drive. Or the two-story, redbrick farmhouse nestled at the top of a rise. Or the way the light rain misted like fog over the green grass of the rolling meadows. Perhaps he couldn't have known how the horses would race to the whitewashed fences beside the barn, almost as if they were welcoming her. Or greeting him, their much-missed friend.

The truck had barely come to a halt before a woman came out of the barn. She was tall and slender, her cloud of dark hair streaked with gray. She walked like Noah, with strong, purposeful strides. Even if she hadn't called out his name and he hadn't hurried from the truck to meet her with a long, affectionate hug, Olivia would have known this was his mother.

Olivia waited in the truck, holding Puddin' and awash with envy. Imagine having a mother who still hugged you like you were six years old.

"Come meet her," Noah said. Olivia sat up straight, suddenly nervous. But instead of bringing his mother over to the truck, Noah took her straight to the trailer. He swung the doors open and let down the ramp while Olivia carried Puddin' around the rig. She paused near the corner as Noah walked Royal Pleasure down.

"Here she is," Noah said proudly to his mother. "Royal Pleasure. Carmen's Best Boy's granddaughter. We've got that bloodline back at last."

"Oh, my," his mother murmured. "Oh, just look at her." Almost reverently she ran her hands over Pleasure's sleek, black coat. "She has the look of Boy, Noah. The same thin, white line down her face. The way her ears are placed. Oh, you pretty, pretty girl. You pretty thing."

Pleasure nickered softly, and Noah's mother laughed, a sweet, musical sound. Olivia thought she was beautiful, standing there in the gentle mist, beaming first at her son and then at the regal, black horse who submitted so willingly to her ministrations.

"She traveled well, didn't..." The woman's voice trailed away as she caught sight of Olivia.

Noah cleared his throat. "There's someone else you should meet."

With a questioning look at her son, his mother stepped forward. "It seems you had another passenger." At Puddin's impudent bark she laughed. "Two other passengers."

Noah introduced them, giving his mother's name as Carmen Raybourne Tremaine.

"Mrs. Tremaine—" Olivia began.

"Call me Carmen, please," the older woman said with a wave of her hand. "And you're Olivia *Franklin?*" Once more she looked expectantly at Noah.

"That's right," he put in. "Franklin, same as the man who sold me Pleasure. Olivia's his daughter."

Carmen was still confused. "And you wanted to see your horse to her new home, Olivia?"

"She's going to work here this summer," Noah explained.

"Work here?" Carmen looked as if a bolt of lightning couldn't have shocked her more. She recovered quickly, however, and held out her hand to Olivia. "Well, my dear, welcome to Raybourne Farms. I wish Noah had called ahead to say you were coming.

I might have prepared a little more. Aired out the guest room.''

''I thought we'd put Olivia in the rooms over the garage,'' Noah said.

''Those rooms have been collecting dust for at least three years,'' Carmen protested.

''A little dust won't hurt anyone.''

''It's more than can be dealt with tonight.'' Firmly Carmen turned back to Olivia. ''Until we get those rooms ready you'll be in the guest room at the main house—that's what we call Noah's place. Let's get your bag.'' She linked her arm though Olivia's. ''I've got dinner started up there.'' Over her shoulder she called, ''We'll eat in forty-five minutes, Son.''

In the space of only a few moments, Olivia was completely enveloped by Carmen's warmth and charm.

Noah watched them go with a sigh. Later, he knew his mother would grill him but good on this situation, and he wasn't sure what he was going to say. That's why he hadn't told her about Olivia when he called last night. She knew he could barely afford the salaries of his trainer and stable boy. So she would have plenty of questions about his bringing another employee home. Noah only hoped he could get away with not telling her about the deal he had made with Olivia's father.

He wasn't sure about that bargain. With each passing mile, Olivia had grown more and more excited about the ''job'' he had given her. He had been deliberately vague when she pressed him for details. Even though he thought the work would do her good, Noah just didn't have the heart to tell her how much time she would spend mucking out stalls and spreading straw.

Cursing himself for getting into this situation, he set about settling Pleasure into her new home. After so many days cooped up in the trailer, he thought she would enjoy a few hours in the fenced yard next to the main barn. That was far enough from the other horses that she wouldn't get spooked, but with enough room to stretch her legs a bit. He would put her in a stall later tonight.

"Tomorrow we'll go for a ride," he promised the mare before leaving her.

With a practiced eye, Noah surveyed the rest of his operation. As he might have expected, his mother and his small staff had the place in perfect order. She had already sent the stable boy, a horse-crazy young neighbor, home for the evening. The pickup belonging to his trainer, Jordan Camp, was missing from its usual place. No doubt the spry old codger had gone off to court his latest paramour, a widow who lived in Murfreesboro.

Outside the barn Noah paused to drink in the familiar sights and sounds. When he considered what Roger Franklin's money would be able to do for the farm, he had to think he had made a good deal, after all. There was so much Noah planned to do.

Had it been only six days since he left? In that short

span of time, the trees had taken on the lushness of summer. The farm looked so damn good. Of course, he loved this place in any season. Dressed in the colors of autumn. With trees stripped bare for the chill of winter. In the delicate, new green of spring. But he thought summer was the farm's most becoming season. The place had a fullness, a ripe texture, as appealing as a woman's curves.

Immediately Olivia popped into his head. Her compact but tantalizing body. Her lusty, uninhibited laughter. Her too-broad smile, which dwarfed her features and yet remained appealing, as well. It suited her. Matched her wild, fiery mane of hair.

How many times between Dallas and Little Rock had he entertained fantasies of running his hands through her hair? From Little Rock to Memphis, he had progressed to imagining burying his face in the fragrant curtain. Beyond Memphis his daydreams had included Olivia, naked in his bed, her hair spread across the pillows, brown eyes slumbery with desire as she looked up at him.

The very thought had him stiff as a poker. Like a stallion sniffing the air for his mate.

He didn't have time for such garbage. Olivia Franklin was off-limits. Her father had asked him to take care of her. Somehow Noah didn't imagine taking her to bed would be an acceptable part of the bargain.

Not that she had given any indication that she was interested. The woman was too involved in things like discovering barbecue sandwiches to notice his covert glances or near-constant state of arousal. Noah had started to think she was as naive as her father had claimed. But she'd been engaged to be married. Surely her fiancé had made her aware of the finer points of the male libido.

"No...ah. Din...ner." The sound of his mother calling him in for the meal snapped Noah from his reverie. He had to grin as she called again, impatient this time. She had called him this way perhaps thousands of times, her voice floating across the meadows, finding him in the midst of mischief or work.

In recent years, they ate together only a few times a week. When Noah had been planning to marry Amy, his mother had decided to move into a small, frame house on another part of the farm, which had once been a sharecropper's residence. He had suggested they switch again when the wedding didn't happen. Carmen had refused. She claimed to like the little house where she gardened and conducted children's piano lessons each afternoon.

So that left him with the redbrick home his grandfather had built over fifty years ago. Square and solid, the house was far from beautiful, but Noah thought it suited the land. When Amy was going to live here, he had taken the time to repair broken shutters and sagging porches and painted the trim a crisp white. Jordan had helped him remodel the kitchen and baths, and had painted and wallpapered much of the indoors according to Amy's specifications.

Since then Noah had ignored the house except as a place to eat and sleep. His mother kept the ivy clipped and the boxwoods tamed and occasionally prodded him into some housekeeping. Noah's money and attention went to the farm.

He reached the screened-in service porch just as his mother stepped up to the door. Puddin' was right behind her, barking a greeting. "We were about to give up on you, Son."

Noah dropped his duffel bag just inside the door and ignored the dog, who was begging for his attention. "I had some things to do."

"They could have waited until after dinner. Now wash up and let's eat," she added, as if he were ten.

Noah caught Olivia's amused glance and scowled. How was he going to exercise any authority if she saw his mother bossing him around like a child?

His attention was caught by Puddin', who had hunkered down on the welcome mat in front of the door. "Looks as if someone has made herself at home."

Olivia chuckled. "She and your cat had a Mexican standoff."

"Mrs. Whiskers retreated upstairs," Carmen said, then gave Noah another reproving look as he started to wash his hands at the sink. "Honestly, Son, Olivia will think I raised you out in the barn. There's a bathroom right down the hall."

"And the water works just fine right here," he retorted. He could see Olivia struggling not to laugh.

"Oh, never mind." Carmen opened the oven and withdrew a pan of evenly browned biscuits. "We're just going to eat in here. You have the dining room table piled high with papers."

"I did the taxes in there instead of down at the office. Haven't had time to clean it up." Noah's chair scraped across the linoleum as he withdrew it from the table. His mother glared at him again.

Olivia, who was already seated, spoke up. "Please, Mrs....Carmen...don't act as if I'm a guest. Remember, I'm working here."

"Yes." Again his mother sent Noah a skeptical glance as she brought the bread basket to the table. She sat, her cheeks rosy from the heat of the oven. "Noah, just what all do you have planned for Olivia to do this summer?"

"There'll be plenty," he said evasively, then surveyed the small, round table with pleasure. "Baked chicken. Fresh peas. Creamed corn. It looks wonderful, Mom."

"Then let's say the blessing." She held out her hands, one to each of them.

Obediently Noah reached for Carmen's and Olivia's hands. Even when their family had been at the lowest point, when the meal was more than likely dried beans and corn bread, his mother had made them all—even his stepfather—clasp hands and give thanks for the bounty of the land.

The ritual was so second nature to Noah that he didn't consider how Olivia might react. He doubted they held hands at the dinner table at the Franklin mansion. When he looked up after his mother's "Amen," Olivia's expression was filled with what he could only describe as wonder. She slipped her hand from his quickly, but he saw that she responded to the squeeze his mother gave her fingers.

"I've been telling Olivia all about the farm," Carmen said as she handed the chicken platter to Noah.

"Seems like that's all I talked to her about during the trip," he said.

Olivia laughed. "You told me about the horses. Your mother's been filling me in on the history."

Spoon poised over the creamed corn, Noah frowned. "What sort of history?"

"Just your family," Olivia retorted with a smile. "Your grandparents coming here to live after the war and such. Your mother said she had never ridden a horse before your father brought her home as his bride."

"I'd never even considered riding." Carmen passed the biscuits and shook her head. "I met Noah's father when he was in the service. I was a big-city girl."

That characterization made Noah chuckle. "My mother grew up in Wichita," he assured Olivia. "A *real* big city."

Carmen laughed, too. "Well, it might not have been a metropolis, but I was more familiar with buses than horses.'' She paused, a fond but sad smile playing about her lips. ''Then your father swept me off my feet.''

''And you learned to ride right away?'' Olivia asked before biting into a flaky biscuit.

''Actually, when we arrived here after his discharge I was pregnant with Noah. His father wouldn't let me near a horse. In those days people were so funny about pregnant women. By the time Charlene came along—''

''Charlene?'' Olivia broke in.

''My daughter,'' Carmen explained.

''You never mentioned your sister,'' Olivia said to Noah.

Softly Carmen said, ''Charly, as we called her, was Noah's half sister. She died almost a dozen years ago, when she was eleven.''

''I'm sorry,'' Olivia murmured.

Carmen brushed her apology aside with an airy wave. ''As I was saying, I rode until I was too big to get into the saddle when I was carrying Charly.'' She bit her lip. ''Sometimes I've wondered if I shouldn't have.''

Noah reached out and touched her arm. ''Mom. Don't go there.''

The exchange heightened Olivia's curiosity. Carmen looked so guilty. Noah so solemn. She had to wonder what had happened to his sister.

The older woman spent the rest of the meal relating amusing tidbits about the farm. Her first misadventures in the saddle. The horse who kept finding ways out of the pastures and onto a neighboring farm. Noah's triumphs in show competitions. Charly wasn't mentioned. Neither was the child's father.

With the skill of a gracious hostess, Carmen soon turned the conversation to their guest. Olivia deliberately glossed over her recently aborted wedding and explained that she wanted to take this summer to discover herself.

"I think I might want to teach," she added as she accepted a slice of chocolate cake and coffee from Carmen. She gave some details about the art education program she had attended in Chicago. "We worked with some children from the community. I loved helping them understand art as an expression of their feelings."

"Are you an artist?" Carmen asked.

Olivia wrinkled her nose. "Not very good, I'm afraid." How was it her father had described her desire to study further after her stint in Chicago? *Rather pointless* was the phrase Olivia thought he had used.

Her attention strayed until she heard Carmen say something about a camp. Vaguely Olivia recalled Noah mentioning that his mother ran a camp of sort.

Carmen leaned forward, warming to her subject. "We started the camp because of Charly. Even with her disability she enjoyed the horses. Riding was such good therapy."

Noah answered Olivia's unspoken question. "Charly had cerebral palsy."

"But she loved being in the saddle," Carmen explained. "She would have stayed outside on a horse all day long. Riding was so good for her that I decided to extend an invitation to other children in the area who were physically or mentally challenged."

Noah got up to refill his coffee cup. "Mother set up a foundation to fund the project. She applies for grants and hits on every bigwig in the state to contribute money." As he leaned against the kitchen counter, the look he sent his mother was warm with pride. "Now every summer, in the middle of July, the farm becomes a day camp."

Olivia was impressed. "It sounds wonderful."

"We do much more than just ride horses," Carmen continued. "There's music, which I oversee. We picnic and sunbathe. Last year we offered art classes, as well. With your training, you'll be a wonderful help with that."

"I don't know that I'm really trained," Olivia said. "But I'm willing to try."

"It's a lot of work," Noah warned.

She stiffened at his implied criticism. "I'm not afraid to work."

"These kids require constant attention and care."

"Of course."

"They don't respond to halfway commitments, and they can smell a rich, fake do-gooder a mile away."

"Noah!" his mother admonished, as Olivia's face colored with anger.

He drained his coffee mug and set it on the counter

with more force than necessary. "I'm sorry." His apology was devoid of sincerity. "Mother, can you show Olivia the guest room. I need to clean out the trailer and put it away."

Without waiting for a reply, he banged out of the screen door. Puddin' came to attention and called after him with short, mournful barks that drew no response.

Olivia released a pent-up breath and tried to smile at the older woman.

"Well," Carmen said after an awkward pause. "It's clear that you are a burr under my son's saddle blanket. I don't like to pry, but maybe you can fill me in."

Though she started out trying to explain just the last four days, Olivia ended up spilling her guts about her whole life. The virtual prison her father had made for her. Marshall. Olivia's plans for independence as a married woman. The wedding. The escape. The capture. Carmen was so easy to talk to that soon Olivia was crying into her coffee as she related how her father had talked to her in that dingy little sheriff's office.

"I've got to show him that I can make it," Olivia said as she accepted a tissue from Carmen and wiped the tears from her cheeks. "He thinks I'm useless and spoiled and stupid. So does Noah." She frowned. "That's why I was so surprised when he offered me a job. He said he wanted to help, to give me a chance to sort things out. But now…'' Puzzled, she stared at the door he had slammed through.

Carmen glanced from the door to her and back again, her expression thoughtful. Slowly she pushed away from the table, stood and started gathering dishes. At the sink she turned and faced Olivia again. ''My son is not an easy person to know or understand.''

Olivia had to laugh. ''Forgive me for agreeing with you.''

''He's been hurt,'' Carmen continued.

''By the girl who left him at the altar?''

His mother seemed surprised. ''He told you about Amy?''

''When he was yelling at me for jilting Marshall, he mentioned he had been in the same situation.''

Shaking her head, Carmen ran water over their plates. ''That nearly killed Noah. But I've never been sure if it was losing her that bothered him so much as the way she did it.''

Olivia stood, walked over to the sink and handed Carmen cups and saucers one by one. ''Noah doesn't take well to people who don't face up to their responsibilities.''

''Oh, no, he doesn't. He can be very hard on people when they fall short of his expectations.'' Carmen pulled open the dishwasher and began stacking the dishes inside. ''I caused him to be that way, I'm afraid.''

Stunned, Olivia almost dropped the cup she was

holding. This woman was the very model of maternal concern and duty. How had Carmen fallen short where Noah was concerned?

"I won't bore you with all the details." Her tone brisk, Carmen continued to fill the dishwasher. "My first husband died when Noah was eight. A short illness. It all happened very fast. We were devastated."

"I understand," Olivia murmured, thinking of her mother's own shockingly sudden death.

"I was frightened. I hate admitting that, but I was. The farm was doing pretty well, but the work was overwhelming. The nephew of one of our neighbors was out of work, and he offered to help. I ended up marrying him. His name was Owen Tremaine."

"That doesn't seem so terrible. You were a young woman. Alone. Lonely."

Sighing, Carmen filled the sink with warm water, adding liquid detergent for bubbles. "It might have been fine if Owen hadn't been such a loser. Although he knew horses, he was lazy. The worst part was that he didn't know how to respond to Noah. The boy just wanted a father. He *needed* a father. But Owen was so hard on him. He said he was trying to make him tough, but I thought he was cruel. I should have followed my instincts and thrown him out the first time we clashed over Noah. But I was pregnant by then, and I kept thinking a child of his own would mellow Owen."

For a moment she stared at the darkened window over the sink, her blue eyes filled with pain. Then she continued, efficiently washing pots and pans as she explained in nearly emotionless tones how the marriage eroded further after Charly was born with so many physical problems. Her husband fell apart, drifting into a gambling addiction she had tried to ignore when they first married. He sold off most of the farm's stock to pay his debts while Carmen went to work as a music teacher in school to pay the bills.

"I let him stay," Carmen said sadly. "And every year he let us down a little more. The end came when he sold Carmen's Best Boy, the horse Noah's father named for me. Noah was sixteen. He just exploded in anger. Owen went after him, and—"

Olivia didn't need the details filled in to understand. She reached out and touched the other woman's arm. "So Owen left."

"And never came back. Not even when Charly died."

"What a jerk."

"He left his mark on Noah," Carmen continued, shaking her head sadly. "He has difficulty trusting anyone. Or accepting shortcomings, in himself or others. And that is my fault, for allowing Owen Tremaine to stay here and damage him that way."

"You were trying to keep a family together," Olivia said. "I know it seems like a mistake now, but weren't you trying to preserve something you thought was important?"

Carmen's tone was dry. "Yes, I took my vows very seriously. I really hoped and tried to make a family with Owen. But when I realized we didn't love each other at all, I should have ended it.''

''Would it have made any difference if you had loved him?''

Head cocked to the side, Carmen studied her. ''That's a very strange thing for a young woman to say. You sound as if you don't believe in love.''

Her back to the counter, Olivia crossed her arms and shrugged. ''To be truthful, I've never given love much thought.''

Carmen burst out laughing. ''A beautiful girl like you, never thinking about falling in love? I can't imagine.''

''I never thought it could happen,'' Olivia said, completely serious. ''I think I always knew my father would pick out someone for me to marry.''

''But in the end you couldn't marry, couldn't pledge yourself to a man you didn't love.''

''My backing out of the wedding wasn't about love,'' Olivia demurred. ''It was about freedom.''

''Maybe,'' Carmen agreed, though her expression contradicted her words.

Before Olivia could protest again, Puddin' barked a warning, Noah opened the door and came in the kitchen. He stopped short, regarding the two women through narrowed eyes. ''What's up?''

''We're just getting acquainted,'' Carmen said, grinning. ''Olivia filled me in on the adventure you two had. You'll have to tell me more some other time, Son.''

His reply was noncommittal, and Olivia added her own giggles to Carmen's.

"I'm glad the two of you are getting along so well." He thrust a weary hand through his hair. "I, for one, am completely exhausted."

"I'm sure." Carmen dried her hands on the dish towel. "I'll leave you to show Olivia her room."

Appearing distressed, Noah demanded, "So you didn't do that already?"

His mother patted him on the cheek. "It is your home, dear. And she is your employee. I'll let you do the honors." She turned and gave Olivia a hug. "I hope I didn't bore you completely."

"Of course not." Olivia returned her embrace with genuine affection. Already she felt as if she had known Carmen for a long, long time.

The older woman touched her cheek. "I think I'm going to enjoy having another woman around to talk with." She gave Noah an impudent glance. "Of course, that's if your boss allows you any time for socializing."

Noah sputtered some sort of reply while Carmen gave Puddin' a pat on the head and disappeared into the soft May evening.

Olivia looked at Noah, and suddenly the kitchen, so spacious only moments ago, shrank. He seemed bigger somehow, broad of shoulder and intensely, completely male. Aside from being bossy, which Olivia had determined was his natural manner, Noah had treated her relatively well during most of their journey. She didn't know why he seemed so irritated with her now.

She cleared her throat in the uncomfortable silence. "Your mother is terrific."

"No argument on that point," Noah murmured. He looked down at Puddin', who was dancing around his feet. "Don't you think you ought to take her outside?"

"I think she just wants you to pick her up."

He grunted and pointedly did not do as the dog so desperately wanted. Instead he gestured toward the hall leading off the kitchen. "Let's give you the grand tour." He picked up his duffel bag and led the way.

The central hallway led from the kitchen and utility rooms, at the rear of the house. The rest of the layout was simple. A bath and large parlor on one side of the hall, a dining room and small, book-lined den on the other. Olivia had little time to register more than comfortable, worn furnishings and neutral, soothing colors before Noah started up the stairs. She retrieved her tote bag from the first step, where Carmen had placed it, and followed him. Puddin' bounded ahead, threatening to entangle herself in Noah's feet at any minute.

The stairway was narrow and dim, with treads that creaked with every other step. So Olivia was pleasantly surprised when Noah flipped a light switch to reveal a cozy landing, complete with a cushioned seat beneath a leaded-glass window. His calico cat, Mrs.

Whiskers, jumped to the floor and slunk down the hall, hissing in Puddin's direction.

"This is her spot," Noah said. "Keep the dog out of it." That, of course, was Puddin's cue to jump into the seat.

Olivia quickly snatched her up, with an apologetic smile at Noah. "This is lovely," she said, gazing around the tiny nook. Muted floral wallpaper in soft blues and greens matched several of the pillows. A stack of books and a wall-mounted lamp added to the cozy appeal.

Noah shot her a challenging look. "What were you expecting?"

"I don't know," she retorted with a smile. "Something more bachelor-like. Dark and gloomy, maybe. Like you pretend to be."

Her feeble attempt at teasing was met with a withering glance as Noah threw open the door to the right of the window seat. "You can sleep here tonight." The overhead light revealed a small, tidy bedroom painted a light blue, with ruffled white curtains at the dormer windows.

Olivia barely had time to digest the essentials before Noah headed down the short hallway. He thumped on a door on the right. "This is the bathroom. There's only one up here, but that shouldn't be a problem since this is only for the night. Tomorrow you'll be over the garage."

She wasn't sure if it was his tone or his expression

that made her future living quarters sound like a death sentence.

Noah thumped the next door on the right. "Towels and other stuff in here. Help yourself."

He backed down the hall, away from her. "I'm going to bed. After you take the mutt out, please lock the kitchen door. We may be out in the country, but we do worry about crime." He pushed open a door to the left and disappeared.

"And that's that," Olivia murmured, looking down at her dog. "I guess we're on our own."

Puddin' yapped a response.

From the room down the hall, Noah called, "I'm a light sleeper. Keep the dog quiet, okay?"

"Yes, sir!" Olivia responded, with as much impertinence as she could muster. She picked up her dog. "Come on, Puddin', let's get ready for bed before our lord and master has us drawn and quartered."

Chapter Five

In his room Noah emptied his bag. Much as he wanted a shower, he didn't head for the bathroom until after he heard Olivia take Puddin' downstairs. His hope was to avoid her as much as possible.

He wasn't sure why he was so irritated with her. She hadn't done anything wrong. Yet he couldn't help wishing she was stowed away in the rooms over the garage.

Someplace where her scent didn't follow him.

Where her laughter couldn't reach him.

Where he couldn't come in a door and find her keeping cozy company with his mother.

He hadn't thought out the logistics of this situation. Every day he was going to have to find something for her to do. Not that there wasn't plenty to accomplish around here, but what was there that a pampered debutante could handle? It was damned hard to imagine her working in the barn all day.

Then there were their living arrangements to consider. She would have to take her meals with him. His mother was busy with her own life. Noah hadn't depended on her for his meals for a long time. His trainer, Jordan, ate by himself in the little trailer where he lived just over the hill. So chances were good Olivia would be at Noah's dinner table every night.

Just him and her.

Very cozy.

Dangerous to his peace of mind.

What the hell was he going to do with her?

A couple of inappropriate answers sprang to mind as he stripped out of his clothes and stepped under the shower spray.

"Hellfire," Noah muttered as his body responded in its usual fashion to such thoughts. He switched the water to cold in hopes of easing his arousal.

"I need to find a willing woman," he muttered as the chilly water sluiced over his body. "I need to just meet somebody and get this out of my system. This is about me being horny. It is not about Olivia Franklin."

As he finished his shower and dried off, Noah decided he would call up that elementary teacher some of his friends had tried to fix him up with in the spring. He'd been too busy to think about a date then. But Saturday he would ask her out, take her to dinner, go back to her place and see what developed.

He went to bed with that plan firmly in mind. At any moment he expected to hear Olivia coming up the stairs. A minute stretched to five, to ten, to thirty. Noah was bone tired. In every aching muscle he could feel the motion of the truck he had been driving for almost a solid week. He needed sleep.

But how the hell could he rest when Olivia was roaming around?

Cursing the very moment she had come into his life, he threw back the covers, jerked on a pair of boxers and stalked down the stairs.

She wasn't anywhere in the house. Noah was starting to worry when he heard a bark from out front. He hurried down the hall, flipped on the outdoor lights and opened the front door. Olivia was curled up with Puddin' in the corner of the front porch swing.

"What in the Sam Hill are you doing?" he demanded.

She blinked, clearly almost blinded by the sudden light. "What do you mean?"

"Were you sleeping out here?"

"Just sitting and enjoying the night air," she replied, still squinting at him. "Why? What's wrong?"

"I didn't know where you were."

Slowly she uncurled her legs. "Did you need me for something?"

Noah figured she couldn't be aware that her rumpled, untucked shirt was held together by only two buttons. Surely she didn't know that when she stretched, she revealed the top of her lacy, white bra and an unsettling amount of plump, tempting cleavage.

With effort, he tore his gaze from that delectable display of flesh. He sounded hoarse, like a desperate man. "Do you know how late it is?"

She squinted at her watch. "Eleven o'clock? Is that late?"

"It is when you have to be up at six."

"Okay, but—"

"And I'm too tired to be awake worrying about where you are."

Her chin snapped up, and she stood. "No one asked you to stay awake and worry."

"When you don't come up to bed, like any normal person, what am I supposed to do?"

"You could think that I was reading. Or watching television. All the things normal people do at night."

"I thought you might be in trouble."

"How?"

"I don't know," he replied. "You could have gone wandering around in the dark. Fell down. Got lost. Any number of things."

A couple of beats passed as she glared at him. "You think I'm that helpless and stupid?"

"Let's say your history doesn't inspire confidence in your judgment."

"My history?" she repeated, her voice shaking.

"You've known me for exactly three days. How can you judge my history?"

"I know enough to realize you need to be looked after."

She sucked in a breath, and when she finally spoke, her voice was low and steady. "I can't believe you. One day you offer me a job and tell me I need a break. You criticize my father for the way he treats me. Now you're treating me the same way. Like I'm some sort of idiot who can't even be trusted to get myself to bed in one piece."

Angrily she pushed past him, reaching for the doorknob. "If you'll excuse me, I'm going to get my things and call a taxi and get out of here before my inherent stupidity causes you any more worry and sleeplessness."

Guilt rocked Noah back on his heels as he blocked the doorway. *Just what was he doing? Venting his frustrations on her?* He took a long, deep breath. Dear Lord, but she was right. He was acting about as reasonable as Roger Franklin. And that was no compliment.

"Let me go," Olivia demanded. "I want out of here."

"And I don't blame you." Moving out of her way, Noah sat down with a heavy sigh in the rocker beside the door.

Olivia hesitated.

"I'm sorry," he told her. "I was out of line to come looking for you. Out of line talking to you like

I did. I understand why you'd like to leave." He managed a wry chuckle. "Only thing is, there's no taxi service out here. So I guess you'll have to walk."

Briefly, she rested her forehead against the door frame and groaned. "A lack of adequate public transportation is going to kill me in the end." Then she turned back to him again. "I really thought you would give me a chance, Noah."

He rested his elbows on the arms of the old chair and stared out at the darkened yard. The rain had ended, and the moon was out, casting the ancient trees and shrubbery in shadow.

"I know you don't like me," she continued.

"It's not that," Noah protested, wondering what she would do if he told her he liked her a little too much, in a most inappropriate way.

"No, you don't." She came around to stand in front of him. "You don't like people who don't pull their weight in the world. Your mother explained some of the reasons why."

His gaze jerked up to meet hers. "What did she say?"

Olivia brushed aside the question. "That doesn't matter. What matters is that I really want to work for you this summer. I want to spend the next couple of months getting my head together, just as you suggested when you offered me the job."

"But maybe now that a few days have passed, if you called your father and went home—"

"I'm not going home," she interrupted, determination in every bone in her body. "Maybe when I know what I want to do with the rest of my life, I'll call my father and let him know where I am and how I'm doing. Right now I just want the job you offered."

"The job thing…well…" Noah cleared his throat and looked up at her, trying to find the words to explain the deal he had made with her father. She would be hurt, yes, but didn't she deserve to know?

"Yes?"

He swallowed hard. He just couldn't tell her. If she found out, he knew she would go running off again. Walking if she had to. She was dead serious about proving herself.

"If you're going to work for me," he continued. "You'd better get some sleep."

Her smile was radiant. "I promise I'm going to do everything you ask. The most menial of tasks. I don't care what you ask of me. I'll do anything for you. Just anything."

Once again Noah had a difficult time keeping his gaze off her gaping shirt, and her offer took on an altogether carnal meaning.

Saturday night, I'm getting some, he promised himself.

Tearing his gaze away from her bosom, he pulled himself out of the chair. "It's late. Call your dog and let's turn in."

Olivia clapped, and Puddin' came bounding across the porch. Straight for Noah.

"Just stop it," he muttered as the pooch stood on her hind legs and began to beg.

"She adores you."

"Hell." Giving in to the animal's insistent pleas, he bent and picked her up. She rewarded him by lathering his face with her rough little tongue. "Oh, jeez, will you take her?"

Laughing, Olivia reached for the dog. Puddin' resisted, determined to stay with Noah. The tussle ended with the dog leaping to the chair and Olivia falling against Noah's chest.

His very bare, very broad, very solid, male chest.

As her hands flattened against his firm, warm flesh, Olivia looked up at him, startled by a jolt of awareness.

Until this moment she had not noticed he wore only a pair of dark-plaid boxers. She had not really looked at the long, finely formed muscles of his chest and arms.

But now, as his hands settled on her shoulders, she took in everything she had missed. Her gaze went to his face, where she encountered a troubled frown.

The question she had been forming died as Noah lifted his hands to her hair. Slowly, gently, he threaded his fingers through one side and then the other, stroking from her scalp to the very ends, which he lifted and allowed to feather down to her shoulders.

He cupped her chin with one strong, work-roughened hand and looked at her with serious, startlingly blue eyes. He spoke as if each word was an effort. "Don't…ever…cut…your…hair."

He was so close. Only a breath away. So close Olivia was certain his mouth would descend toward hers. And how she wanted him to kiss her. Olivia was certain she had never wanted anything more than she wanted to feel Noah Raybourne's lips move across hers.

But he released her. He stepped into the house with a mumbled good-night.

Olivia remained on the porch, one hand pressed to the lips he hadn't kissed. She was so confused. One moment the man acted as if he couldn't stand her. Then he touched her. He almost kissed her.

What exactly did Noah Raybourne want from her?

Taking pity on Olivia, Noah waited until 7:00 a.m. before he banged on her bedroom door the next morning. He heard the dog bark, Olivia curse and something hit the floor. Then she jerked open the door, bleary-eyed and wrapped in a blanket, with that glorious red mane of hers in tangled disarray.

Her fresh-from-bed, innocent appeal would have sent him running for cover if he weren't determined to pretend he didn't care.

He said, "Rise and shine, Princess. The workday started over an hour ago."

She groaned and slammed the door. But a half hour later she was in the kitchen, bathed and bright-eyed.

Noah was determined to act as if last night had not

happened. He felt like an absolute fool for having given in to the urge that had nagged at him ever since she had unbraided her hair. So now he knew. Her hair was as pleasurable to touch as to look at. His unreasonable attraction to her had to end right there.

He tried to tell himself there was nothing too expectant in Olivia's gaze this morning. He didn't need her soft and womanly smile. He certainly didn't need her treating him as if they shared a secret. What he needed was to make sure there were no opportunities for further meetings on moonlit porches.

He was going to do just as her father had asked. The princess was about to find out just how tough a world without housekeepers and maids could be. If he made it tough enough, maybe she would scurry on home to Daddy. At this point Noah thought he would gladly pay Franklin for Royal Pleasure and forfeit the promised money.

He pointed to the juice, cereal and coffee on the counter. "Get yourself something to eat. Then come out to the garage. You can get started on where you're going to live."

Once he had disappeared into the bright, morning sunshine, Olivia leaned over to wrinkle her nose at Puddin'. "That didn't go exactly the way I planned."

Olivia had lain awake half the night, reliving that moment on the porch. She figured that in her inexperience she had done something wrong. Clearly, Noah had sent her some sort of signal, and she had messed up the reply. That's why he hadn't kissed her.

This morning she planned to dazzle him with her smile. Be a little flirtatious. See how he reacted. He hadn't even noticed.

It wasn't as if she had never been kissed. There had been dates, although generally supervised by a "suit." So they were pretty tame. And with Marshall...well, he had been very respectful, even on those few occasions when they were completely alone. He certainly had kissed her, touched her. But never, not once, had he made her feel half of the yearning she had experienced last night with Noah.

This was not good.

Especially since Noah now acted as if she was no more attractive than any other employee.

"I don't understand men," she told Puddin'. From outside, she heard Noah calling her name, and she gulped down a last swallow of orange juice. "I especially don't understand that man."

She and Puddin' trotted across the yard to the garage which sat a short distance to the rear of the house. An outside flight of stairs led to an open door, from which sizable clouds of dust were billowing.

Gingerly they climbed the steps and paused in the doorway. Noah was energetically beating dust out of the yellowing curtains. An older man, who reminded Olivia of nothing so much as a wizened gnome, stood to the side, shaking his head.

Coughing, Olivia took in the dreary room. A brown tweed sofa was flanked by mismatched end tables, neither of which went with the glass-topped coffee table. A sagging blue recliner and a couple of lamps completed the living room furniture. An alcove sported a bed with a definite dip in its midsection and a scarred dresser with a broken mirror. A half-open door led to what Olivia imagined was the bathroom. Water spots decorated the ceiling. Peeling paint covered the wall. Cracked linoleum was on the floor. Dirt covered everything.

"I know it looks bad," Noah said, giving up his curtain beating to face her. "But I put a new roof on the place last summer, so the leaks are stopped." He pointed to the brown water spots. "The air-conditioning unit still works, too." He indicated a window unit that looked like nothing Olivia had ever seen before.

Almost proudly, Noah stood in the center of the room and made a slow turn. "Once you get it clean, this will be a nice little place. I lived up here one summer when I was wanting some privacy. And I had a hired man who stayed here a couple of years back."

The older man spoke up for the first time, the words forced out around the tobacco bulging in his cheek. "Yep, that hired man lasted about two weeks up here." He regarded Olivia with dark eyes that fairly danced with merriment in the midst of his wrinkled face.

"This is Jordan, my trainer," Noah said by way of introduction. "And this is Olivia, the woman I told you was going to be working for us this summer."

Jordan dipped his head in greeting. "I'm pleased to meet you, ma'am."

She murmured a response, still too overwhelmed by this horrible room to say very much. Puddin' wouldn't even cross the threshold. Looking around in horror, Olivia couldn't blame her. She stared at Noah. "You honestly expect me to live here?"

His face hardened. "It won't be so bad when you get it cleaned up."

She swallowed hard, thinking of the clean, comfortable room he had given her last night. "I don't believe this place will come clean."

"Sure it will." He began jerking the curtains down. "You can wash these—" The words were cut short when the rotting fabric gave way and ripped down the middle.

Jordan was consumed by a fit of coughing that Olivia was sure masked laughter.

But without missing a beat, Noah tossed the ruined curtains into the corner. "Maybe Mom has some old curtains you can put up here."

Olivia tried to think of something to say. Something hopeful or positive. But she was worried that if she tried to talk, she'd dissolve into a weak bout of tears.

"You'll find all the cleaning stuff you need in the utility room off the kitchen at the house," Noah added. "Mops. Soap. Bleach for the bathroom. You'll have it shipshape in no time. When you're finished, we'll get you started out at the barn. There's plenty for you to do out there, too.''

Again Jordan was seized by a coughing fit. With a last nod at Olivia, he left, and the coughs turned to guffaws on the outside staircase.

"Don't mind him," Noah told her. "He can be a real character." He breezed past Olivia and whistled as he clambered down the steps. Puddin' was still rooted to the threshold, as if in shock. Olivia's hands were trembling. She eased down onto the arm of the threadbare couch and bit her lip.

Then she heard Noah shout her name. Certain he was going to tell her these living quarters were a joke, she hurried out to the stair's landing.

He stood on the back porch of his house, shaking a bottle of orange juice. "One thing you better learn, Princess. You don't leave food sitting out to ruin. There's no maid here to clean up after you!" He went inside, slamming the door.

Olivia retreated, as well. To the center of the brown-spotted, filthy room where she was expected to live for the next several months.

"I won't," she told Puddin'. "I'll just march down there and tell him I won't."

That was exactly what her father would expect her to do. Run screaming at the first obstacle.

Noah expected it, too, she'd bet. He was planning to gloat when she refused the first task he assigned her. That's why he'd been calling her "princess" all morning with that rotten smirk on his mouth.

She had only one choice.

She had to show everyone she could do this.

Including herself. *Most importantly* herself.

Olivia straightened her shoulders and started for the door. "Come on, Puddin'. We've got work to do."

"I think you are positively cruel," Noah's mother told him. Arms folded, she stood on the screened porch of his house and gazed toward the garage. She had brought some chicken salad and apple pie for lunch and learned what he had Olivia doing.

He laughed. "She's got to have a place to live."

"She could stay here with you."

"Not a good idea."

Carmen regarded him with frank speculation. "You're very attracted to her, aren't you?"

Sex wasn't a subject Noah was in the habit of discussing with his mother. "Please," he said with a dismissive gesture. "She's a social princess. And you know my track record where that sort of woman is concerned."

His mother was not to be put off. "I didn't ask if you thought she was suitable for you. I asked if you were attracted to her. One thing doesn't necessarily have anything to do with the other."

"Mom, just stop it. I'm not interested in that woman."

"Then explain to me again why she's here."

Carmen had demanded to hear his side of the story behind Olivia's presence at the farm. Noah had concocted a tale that didn't include Roger Franklin giving him anything in exchange for a summer spent riding herd on his daughter. Carmen would never understand nor condone such an arrangement, especially since it involved deceiving Olivia. So Noah had simply told her he felt sorry for Olivia and truly wanted to give her a job and a chance to sort through her life. None of which was untrue. He avoided any explanation of how he was going to pay her.

"I couldn't just leave her sitting at that bus station," Noah now explained to his mother once again. "This is a woman who doesn't know the first thing about taking care of herself. Who knows what kind of trouble she might have found herself in."

Carmen directed a concerned glance toward the garage apartment. "I'm sure Olivia feels as if she's in deep trouble right now."

"A little elbow grease never hurt anyone. If so, you would have killed me several times over before I was ten."

"But still—" Again his mother looked toward the garage with worry. "I hope she knows what she's doing. Has she ever cleaned before?"

Thinking of the milk and juice she had left on the counter, Noah shook his head. "I'm sure she's never done anything more strenuous than her nails."

"Then I'm going to check on her. She might mix bleach and ammonia, inhale the fumes and pass out." Ignoring his protests, Carmen started across the yard. She was halfway to the garage when a scream rang out. Then another. And another. Each more blood-curdling than the last and underlined by Puddin's frantic barks.

Noah hadn't moved so fast since he lettered in track. He passed his mother, raced up the stairway and met Olivia on her way out. What skin he could see beneath the grime covering her face was white.

He grabbed her by the shoulders. "What is it? What's wrong?"

Olivia pointed inside. "Puddin' has them. I'm not sure…I think they're…"

Charging inside, Noah found Puddin' barking her head off in the corner beyond the sofa where she had penned a family of field mice.

"It's only mice," Noah shouted, relieved to see the dog wasn't tangling with something more vicious.

Carmen, who had reached the top of the stairs, slipped her arm around Olivia's shoulders. "Only mice? Son, there's no such thing. Get those nasty things out of there. And figure out how they got in."

"Maybe this broken window," he said, studying the missing pane in the window over the couch.

"Make sure nothing worse is in there," Carmen instructed.

"Worse?" Olivia demanded. "I've already fought off spiders, bugs and lizards. What else could there be?" Frantically she called for her dog.

"Spiders, bugs and lizards. Fought them all with-out screaming for help." Carmen patted her on the shoulder and grinned in triumph at Noah. "I'd say that's pretty darn good."

Olivia shivered. "I just couldn't take the mice."

"Well, Noah's going to deal with them right now. You come on down and have some lunch."

"Take your dog," Noah yelled after the women. Olivia called, but Puddin' stubbornly refused to leave his side.

"Useless creature," Noah muttered. Only grudgingly did he admit that the animal helped as he trapped the mice in a box. He wedged a piece of cardboard over the missing windowpane and, much to Puddin's dismay, he let the mice go behind the garage.

Moments later he carried the dusty-haired mutt onto the screened-in porch, where his mother and a clean-faced Olivia were sharing lunch at a table. "This dog does not belong outdoors."

"Of course she doesn't," Olivia said, taking the dirty creature in her arms. "But I didn't want to leave her here in the house to bother your cat."

"We'll put Mrs. Whiskers up in the apartment. She'll find anything else that's hiding up there." Grinning at Olivia's shiver, he went inside to wash his hands.

He heard his mother soothe her. "Dear, I promise you nothing is going to harm you in that apartment."

When he returned with his lunch, his mother sported what he had come to know as her "take no prisoners'' look. "Noah, Olivia is not moving into that place until it's fit for her to live in."

"She's working on getting it clean." In fact, Noah had been impressed by how much she had accomplished this morning.

"Not just clean. I want those water stains repaired, the walls painted—"

"Now wait a minute—"

"I won't have her treated badly while she's here."

"But I don't have time—"

"If you don't make time, I'll just have to find room for her at my place, though goodness knows where—"

"Wait just a minute!" Olivia's interruption forced them both to look at her. Her mouth was set in a stubborn line. "Carmen, it's nice of you to stick up for me, but it's not necessary. And I'm not going to intrude on your privacy. I'm going to get the rooms over the garage livable. By tonight."

"But, dear, you can't—"

"Yes, I can," she insisted, raising her chin. "I may not get it painted and replastered, but it is going to be clean. The only thing I ask is that Noah make sure there's not some other hole where creatures are getting in."

Still looking reluctant, Carmen glared at him. "That's the least you can do."

He agreed. And he couldn't help regarding Olivia with admiration. He would believe her sleeping up there when he saw it, but he had to give her points for working hard. After lunch he checked the place out for varmint entry points, then replaced the broken pane of glass and left Mrs. Whiskers on mouse and lizard patrol. Olivia got on with her formidable task.

Noah had plenty of work to keep him busy, but that didn't stop him from checking on Olivia from time to time. She scrubbed and mopped. She attacked the stained sink, toilet and shower with bleach. She turned over the couch and the chair to root out any lingering pests. She washed the walls and the windows. She polished the living area's ancient light fixture. She dragged the mattress out and propped it on the stair landing to air in the warm sunshine. Then she threw the ugliest of the two end tables in the garbage. Long after he figured she would give up, she stuck to the work.

About five o'clock Carmen arrived with an old rag rug, a set of curtains, some bed linens, pillows and an assortment of other supplies. The paint was still peeling, and the water spots were still glaringly ugly, but when Noah peeked in around dinnertime, he had to admit the place was livable. He left his mother and Olivia making the bed and went to prepare dinner.

Olivia almost fell asleep over the steak he grilled.

But after they had eaten and Carmen had departed, she insisted on washing the dishes. Or at least she attempted to stack them in reasonable order in the dishwasher. Noah showed her how they should be arranged. By that time Olivia was swaying on her feet.

Noah felt a definite kick of guilt. "You're done in," he said, and took away the grill she was attempting to dry. "I'll get these last few things."

Olivia dragged a hand through hair still damp from the shower she had taken before dinner. She wasn't certain she would ever feel clean again. "I'll go up and get my things and then head out to my new place."

She caught Noah's slight hesitation. A part of her wished he would tell her to stay there just one more night. But another part of her knew she couldn't do that. She had made her lumpy, caved-in bed, and it was out over the garage where she would have to lie in it.

She gathered her clothes and toiletries and came back to the kitchen to collect Puddin'. The dog and Mrs. Whiskers had declared a truce and were both asleep under the kitchen table.

"Let me get her," Noah said, when Olivia groaned as she started to bend.

"Thanks. Every muscle in my body is going to stiffen up tonight."

"I have something you could rub..." Noah's words trailed away.

Olivia had the feeling that both of them were screening the same mental image—him massaging her tired and aching back. She experienced the same jolt of awareness that had arced between them last night. Surely he felt it, too.

With undue haste, he shifted her dog into her arms. Avoiding her gaze, he also held out a key ring.

She looked up, puzzled.

"It's for the doors," he muttered. "The small one fits the rooms over the garage. The bigger one is for here. In case you...well, in case you need something."

Her gaze narrowed. "I suppose you think I'll be scurrying back over here pretty fast."

"I didn't say that."

"You didn't have to." Olivia plucked the keys from his palm and headed for the door. She called an airy, deliberately casual good-night and walked out. She made it all the way to her new home without looking back.

Inside, she gazed with dismay at the moths buzzing around the overhead light. She sighed at the steady *drip-drip* of the leaking faucet in the bathroom. She groaned as Puddin' jumped up and padded across the bed, leaving dirty tracks on the clean, white spread Carmen had brought.

But not once did she think of beating a retreat across the yard.

She would show Noah Raybourne she was made of tougher stuff than he imagined.

She had to wonder, if and when he no longer regarded her as a princess, would he act on the awareness that had sprung up between them?

"For God's sake," Olivia muttered. "I have lost my mind." Didn't she have enough problems without worrying whether that stubborn, bossy man found her attractive? For starters, she had to somehow make it through her first night in this hell-hole.

After dropping her things on the couch, she brushed her teeth and climbed in between the lumps and the sag and her already-snoozing dog. "I'll never get to sleep," she told the stain on the ceiling.

That was her last thought before noise jolted her awake. Someone was pounding on her door. Noah was calling her name. It was too dark to be morning already. Something must be wrong.

Muscles screaming in protest, she stumbled to the door and swung it open. Sure enough, Noah stood on the stairway landing.

His grin was as infuriating as his greeting. "Morning, Princess. Rise and shine. We're going to have to find you an alarm clock."

As he turned to go, Olivia briefly considered giving him a kick to his jeans-clad rear. She might have done it if the rear in question weren't too damned appealing to injure in a tumble down the stairs. She settled for enjoying the view before she slammed her door and faced day number two as a working woman.

Chapter Six

"How's it going?"

"Slow," Olivia replied, looking up from oiling a saddle to grin at the lanky fifteen-year-old who had popped into the Raybourne Farms tack room. Cody was the farm's part-time stable boy and her partner in all tasks smelly or downright nasty. In the two weeks since she had come to work, he had proven to be a staunch ally.

Cody ducked his shaggy dark head and sighed. "At least you're inside. It is really hot out there today."

"Is June always this humid?"

"Just wait until August," he said, braces flashing as he laughed. He sobered suddenly, an ear cocked to the side. "Uh-oh, I think Noah's coming. I'd better get back to work on the fences I'm repairing."

Olivia waved goodbye, then reapplied herself to the saddle. Once upon a time she had regarded horses as elegant and patrician companions, somewhat regal and mysterious. But after nearly two weeks at Raybourne Farms, her perspective had changed quite a bit.

Now she knew that behind every horse were hours of backbreaking labor. She had cleaned dirty stalls, gagging over the smell. She had hauled blocks of hay and bags of feed, groaning under the load. She knew exactly which muscles ached the most after grooming an excitable yearling. She smelled like liniment, had saddle oil under her fingernails and the sprinkle of freckles across her nose had bloomed into a full-fledged garden.

As low man in the organizational structure of the farm, she was privileged—or was it burdened?—to experience the gritty side of caring for a stable of expensive horseflesh. As a result, she had a new appreciation for the men and women who had once trotted out prettily groomed and perfectly saddled horses for her pleasure. In fact, when she could afford it, she planned to send the entire stable staff at her father's ranch a huge present. While she didn't think she had ever been ungrateful for their efforts, she knew now just how hard they worked.

She was proud to say she was sticking with the work, as well. From stable work to housework, she had not given up on anything Noah asked of her. She didn't always get it right, but no one could say she didn't try. Cody had helped, with his boundless good humor. Jordan, the trainer, was a dear, as well. Olivia had forgiven him the way he had laughed at her predicament that first morning in the rooms over the garage. He was a salty and irreverent old flirt, fond of calling her "Livvie" and complimenting her when she knew she looked her sweatiest, grungiest worst.

Jordan and Cody had joined Carmen in lifting Olivia's spirits when she could have felt quite lost. More important, however, was the satisfaction she had found in being busy and productive. She didn't kid herself that the work was world changing, but everything she learned was another step toward self-sufficiency and independence. She experienced a quiet thrill in completing each task, a pride that nothing in her privileged, protected and empty life had brought her before.

Most days Noah gave her grudging approval. From time to time, he forgot to be aloof and boss-like and even managed to smile and talk to her. Sometimes he even seemed glad she was here.

Just yesterday morning she had been working with Jordan to smooth out the canter of one of Noah's fillies. The canter was the "rocking chair" gait for which Tennessee Walking Horses were famous. Everything had clicked, with the animal turning in a show-ring-perfect performance under Olivia's guidance. Noah had been so excited when Olivia dismounted, he caught her up and swung her around and around. She had been breathlessly aware of their closeness. The strong muscles that lifted her. His big hands on her waist. His face just inches from her own.

Then she had looked into his deep, blue eyes and watched the laughter fade. He had set her down and stepped away with a mumbled apology. Confused, Olivia could only watch him walk away.

Turning, she had found Jordan grinning at her in pleased and knowing delight. "Oh, stop it," she had ordered as she stalked back to the horse.

Jordan had cackled. "Don't be discouraged, Livvie. Even the randiest of studs sometimes resist their natural inclinations."

Heat suffused her face. "I don't know what you mean."

"Oh, but I think you do," Jordan retorted with yet another cackle. "I think you do."

Of course Olivia knew. There was an electricity in the air between her and Noah that was hard to miss. While she wasn't opposed to investigating it further, Noah was bound and determined to ignore it. She wished she could ignore him. She wished she could stop seeking him out or craving his approval. But for some reason what he thought mattered to her very much.

"Hey, Princess!"

His shout made Olivia groan. She had known he would come to see if she was finished with the tack. Nothing around this place escaped Noah's notice for long. Not a buckle unpolished, a floor unswept or a light left on.

"Princess!"

"In here!" she shouted back, not bothering to hide her aggravation. "And the name's not Princess!"

He swung open the door without acknowledging her usual admonition. "Aren't you finished?"

"No." Grimacing, she straightened from her tedious work. "And I won't be finished until nearly dinnertime."

Noah strolled over to survey her work and gave what sounded like a grunt of approval. "You've got that old saddle looking pretty good. But you needn't put so much time into it."

"You told me you wanted everything in this room in top shape. Jordan showed me what had to be done."

"I didn't know it would take you all week."

She resisted the urge to toss her oily rag into his handsome face. Couldn't he lighten up a little?

It wasn't just Olivia he was on to every minute. He rode everyone hard. Cody, who would most likely give his arm for him. He even chastised Jordan, who was old enough to be Noah's grandfather and had once worked for his father. About the only person Noah didn't yell at regularly was his mother, and Olivia figured that was because Carmen would yell back.

It was difficult to resent Noah too much, because he worked himself hardest of all. Though Olivia had trained herself to rise at five-thirty every morning, he was always in the kitchen before her, brewing coffee and gearing up for the day. He worked at top speed from dawn till dusk. Exercising stock. Laying in supplies. Directing Cody in repairs and unending renovation projects. Working with Jordan on the mounts they were training for competition. Answering inquiries on the yearlings he had for sale or the stallions available for stud. And showing Olivia, sometimes over and over again, what he needed her to do.

Most nights he spent in his office. On her regular evening strolls with Puddin', Olivia had glimpsed him through the lighted window of his office in the stable. Just last night she had stood in the moist evening air, watched him rub his eyes and briefly bury his face in his hands. The gesture lasted only a moment. He was soon glaring at his computer screen again, but it had made Olivia's chest tighten.

He had looked so worried. So alone. Very different from the hard-driving, in-control man she usually saw. She had wanted to go in and ask him what was wrong and if she could help, but she had backed away, knowing he wouldn't appreciate her nosing in on his business.

Now she bit back an acid-tinged retort to his criticism of the pace of her work. Picking up her rag again, she turned the conversation to farm business. "Does the breeder from Kentucky want the chestnut yearling?"

"No."

She was astounded. Noah had spent most of yesterday afternoon showing off a horse named Cotton's

Pride for the owner of a Kentucky farm. "But why?"

His face hardened. "He said my price was too steep. I couldn't back down. Not and turn any profit."

Biting her bottom lip, Olivia gave the saddle one last rub. Then she looked up at Noah. "I'm really sorry."

His shrug was a shade too casual. "There'll be another buyer."

"I know, but…" From Jordan, she knew Noah had been counting on this sale. Money problems might be at the root of the despair she had glimpsed last night through his office window. It seemed inadequate, but all she could do was offer another "I'm sorry."

Noah's gaze caught hers and held. For a moment she thought he was going to say something more. When he didn't, she was left with the usual frustration. Just when it seemed he might reach out to her, he always pulled back. She was crazy for letting it bother her.

"See if you can't get the rest of this tack up to snuff today, Princess."

The hated nickname made her groan. She spread her arms, then gestured toward her stained T-shirt and jeans. "Do I look like a princess?"

Noah's mouth went dry. She looked…sexy. A flame-haired siren slumming in blue jeans. Her appeal wasn't dimmed by the dirty clothes she sported most days. Her face was most often glowing with sweat, not expensive cosmetics. The crowning beauty of her hair was invariably in braids or caught up in a ponytail, as it was now. The pungent smell of horseflesh and hay had replaced the expensive perfume she had been wearing the first time they met.

But every day she looked better to him than any woman had looked in a long, long time. Much, much better than the attractive kindergarten teacher he'd taken out—and not even kissed—last Saturday night. Better than anyone since the woman who had left him standing at the altar.

Tempting as Olivia was, however, she was still a princess. Two weeks of manual labor and sleeping over the garage had not changed that she was a woman as unsuited to him and his way of life as a Thoroughbred mated to a plow horse. Every time he thought about responding to the little flares of interest she directed his way, he reminded himself what a boatload of trouble he would buy by getting involved with her.

That's what he thought of now as he cleared his throat. "Just get back to work, *Princess*. And don't forget you're cooking tonight."

She groaned. "Oh, God. Let's hope I get it right. I'm starving."

"I thought you were going to stick to something safe, like spaghetti out of a jar."

"You know I might ruin that, too."

Noah fought to suppress a grin. Olivia had surprised him by offering to take over some of the cooking chores, a duty he was glad to pass on. But burned hamburgers and a pizza still frozen in the center had been the result of her efforts thus far. He and his mother had shown her some basics, but she seemed to be catching on at the barn faster than in the kitchen.

"I can do dinner tonight if you want," he offered. "I'm hungry, too."

Her mouth set in the stubborn line he was beginning to know very well. "No, I'll do it. Dinner at six-thirty sharp."

Resigning himself to another meal of canned soup and cold sandwiches, he headed to his office across the corridor from the tack room. He closed the door and sat down at his desk. Almost reluctantly he unlocked the top drawer. From an envelope, he withdrew a check, the one Olivia's father had written in that sheriff's office in Texas.

Five thousand dollars, paid in gratitude for the trouble she had caused him. Franklin had said this money was his, free and clear, no matter if Olivia stayed the summer or not. Yet Noah hadn't been able to bring himself to cash the check. It still seemed dishonest, somehow. But God knew the farm could use the money.

With a sigh, he picked up the business card Franklin had given him. Franklin wanted regular reports on Olivia. Noah took a deep breath and reached for the phone. Evidently, Franklin had given his secretary instructions to put Noah straight through when he called. The man came on the line immediately.

"So my daughter is safe." It was a statement, not a question.

Noah's eyes narrowed. "Either you have no doubts about my integrity or you're having us watched."

"Right on both counts," Franklin retorted.

Anger roughened Noah's voice. "If you already know how she is, then I'll save on my phone bill by hanging up."

"No, wait a minute." Franklin paused.

"Yes?" Noah prompted. "I've got better things to do than hang on the phone."

The man at the other end of the line cleared his throat. "I wanted to know…umm…how is she?"

"Like you said. Safe."

"But she's…okay?"

Noah released an impatient breath. "Are you wondering if she's homesick? Does she talk about you? Does she seem ready to run home?"

There was silence from Franklin's end.

Noah gave a mirthless laugh. "The answer is no. Even with all the gritty, dirty work I've thrown at her, she hasn't said a word about you or about going home. She's making it just fine without you to guide her every movement." He found himself gloating, even though Olivia's departure was something he had hoped for.

Franklin's voice was full of pretense. "Well that's good news. Good for you, Raybourne. You'll be getting that bonus check if this keeps up."

"I haven't cashed the first check," Noah pointed out.

"You will."

Noah slammed the phone down on the man's chuckle. He wasn't going to call him again. If Franklin wanted to know how Olivia was, then his spying henchmen would just have to give him reports. Or he could call her himself. What Noah ought to do was tear the man's check up and mail it back to him right now.

But, instead, Noah left it just where it was. He sat for a moment, staring at the phone and cursing the day he ever got involved with Franklin. Then he turned to his computer and flipped to his financial statement. Unfortunately, the spreadsheet on this month's expenses looked just the same as last night. He had counted on the sale of Cotton's Pride to make up for the shortfall.

The picture changed if he added in the check for Royal Pleasure, which Franklin was holding. Noah tapped a few keys. Then he added the five thousand dollars resting in his drawer. Then five thousand more for Olivia lasting the rest of the summer. Those figures made a big difference in his bottom line.

But he didn't know if he could ever cash that check in his drawer. He certainly couldn't count on getting the money for Pleasure back from Franklin. Stubborn as Olivia had turned out to be, she could still bolt at any moment. Hell, he had done everything he could to drive her away. Sooner or later she might take him up on it.

Noah removed the extra money from his financial statement and flipped off the computer. His problems really had nothing to do with Franklin or Olivia. He had caused them himself. By wanting Royal Pleasure.

That was his folly. In his eagerness to get his hands on the bloodline that had been his father's pride, the bloodline Owen Tremaine had sold, Noah had gambled with his financial stability. Seventeen years after Owen had left them high and dry, after all the work he and his mother had put into rebuilding this place, Owen still impacted Noah's decisions. It was stupid. And yet...

Wheeling his chair around, Noah gazed at the framed photographs that covered the opposite wall. They showed his grandparents, his father and mother and himself with a succession of horses. Prize-winners and champions. Prime breeding stock sought out by breeders, dealers and horse enthusiasts throughout the country. No, they had never been rich. Their operation had remained small when compared to some of the big breeders, like his ex-fiancée's father. But Raybourne Farms had carved out a place of respect in the world of the Tennessee Walking Horse.

In a fit of rage over something Noah had or hadn't done, Owen had once torn all these photographs down and thrown them in the garbage. Noah and his mother had picked them out, cleaned them off and hidden them from view. The pictures went back up on this wall the day Owen left for good. Noah could remember standing here, sixteen years old and scared to death that his stepfather's debts would force them off the land that was his birthright. He had determined then that he was going to set to rights what Owen had tried to ruin.

That's why he had wanted Pleasure. To restore what had been lost. He would breed her to his best stallion, Smoky's Delight. He had no doubt the result would be the catalyst for the kind of success he wanted for his farm.

"Buying Pleasure wasn't a mistake," he muttered. Somehow he would guide the farm through their temporary cash-flow difficulties. Filled with new resolve, he reached for the card file on his desk. He needed to let some other farms know that Cotton's Pride was still for sale. Even without Franklin's money, this farm was going to survive.

Olivia stepped back from the table, then leaned forward again to rearrange the bouquet of wildflowers. Carmen had brought them by, along with freshly ground oregano. She had assured Olivia that the herb, which she grew herself, would perk up the bottled spaghetti sauce.

All Olivia hoped for was that she didn't do something stupid. She turned to check the stove. The sauce, with chunks of sausage added, was warming on the lowest heat. Water was bubbling in anticipation of the noodles. The salad was chilling in the refrigerator, and bread was buttered and ready to go into the preheated oven. She checked the temperature one more time. The oven setting was what had tripped her up with the frozen pizza she had tried for her last meal with Noah.

"Even I can't screw this up," she murmured.

Puddin's bark was no reassurance at all. The dog's new best friend, Mrs. Whiskers, offered her own candid meow.

"You two have no faith in me whatsoever, do you?"

As if in answer, the animals retreated to their favorite positions under the table. They reminded her of a theater audience getting set for a performance.

Choosing to ignore them, Olivia crossed to the mirror hanging on back of the utility room door and checked her reflection for about the tenth time. She scowled at what she saw. Last week she had gone into Murfreesboro with Carmen and picked up a few more clothes and other necessary items, again at a discount store. Not wanting to spend much of her stash of cash or the meager salary she had earned thus far, she had stuck with practical purchases. Now she wished for something a little dressier than the navy shorts and striped knit top she had already worn several times.

But the problem with her looks wasn't just her clothes. The shower she had taken had combined with the humidity to turn her hair into a riot of kinky curls. And as for her skin… The dermatologist she had regularly seen in Austin would have a stroke at her freckles and the size of her pores. The bare essential cosmetics she had stuffed in her tote when she'd left the ranch did little to improve the situation.

"I look terrible," she muttered. "Why should Noah—"

She cut off the question before she could ask it. Just a few hours ago at the barn she had promised herself she wouldn't think about Noah as anything but her boss. She was determined to squash any undue interest in the shape of his buns or the length of his legs or the deep, deep blue of his eyes. She was going to ignore any little thrill of pleasure that might come over her if he smiled in her direction.

He had made it very clear he wasn't interested in her as anything but an employee. And that was fine. She should be grateful. The last thing she needed was to jump into some kind of reckless romance. She needed to sort out her life, not fall in love.

So why was she sweating over her looks and obsessing about his dinner?

Instead of answering that question, she turned from the mirror, checked the sauce again and gave it a sprinkle more of oregano. It had been sweet of Carmen to bring this by and to help Olivia sauté the Italian sausage.

The older woman had tactfully said nothing about the tablecloth Olivia had unearthed from a drawer in the dining room breakfront. Or the carefully set table. Or Olivia's obvious nerves. But such cordial respect was what Olivia had learned to expect from Noah's mother. Carmen seemed to accept that Olivia was an adult. She treated her son the same way. For someone who had grown used to a parent who couldn't let go, even for a moment, the situation was quite refreshing.

Smiling, Olivia went over and straightened the flowers once more. If horse dung was her least favorite part about coming to Raybourne Farms, then Carmen was her favorite.

Or maybe her second favorite, she amended a moment later, as Noah came in the door.

He was a mess: his recently shorn, light-brown hair in disarray; his jeans dusty; and his plain, blue work shirt dark with sweat at the collar and under the arms. Most women of Olivia's acquaintance wouldn't see past his workingman's clothes. Maybe she would have done the same a few weeks ago. But now she looked at Noah and her breath seemed to catch in her chest.

Telling herself to get a grip, she managed a smile. "I think I've made a dinner we can actually eat."

"Yeah…" Noah's gaze traveled from her to the well-set table to the pans on the stove and then back again. Their eyes met and he looked away. "Is there time for me to shower? I got caught up helping Cody clean out a fence row."

Olivia nodded. "I'll just wait to cook the pasta. Your mother said seven minutes."

With a nod, Noah headed upstairs, trailed by Puddin' and Mrs. Whiskers, his adoring fans.

Olivia sat down to wait and tried not to think about him just one floor above, shucking his clothes, muscles flexing as he stepped into the shower. She wondered what it would be like to just walk in the bathroom, pull back the shower curtain and take full measure of him. She pictured Noah grinning and then holding out his hand....

For someone who had never given much thought to sex, Olivia realized she was developing quite a rich and varied fantasy life. Each and every scenario starred Noah and her in various states of undress, and each scene was less likely to happen than the one before.

She had composed her wayward thoughts by the time Noah came downstairs. Well scrubbed, in jeans and a white polo shirt, he was more attractive than ever. Yet she managed to put the bread in the oven to toast and cooked the pasta without drifting off into fantasy land.

Noah complimented the food and asked for seconds. They fell into an easy conversation about the horses and his plans for shows this fall. Things were going fine until a smoky, burned aroma began to permeate the kitchen.

Olivia put a hand to her mouth. "I forgot the bread."

Noah reached the oven before her, flipped open the door and rescued a tray of blackened chunks.

"Just look at that," she muttered. "Tell me how anyone ever gets a whole dinner on the table."

"We didn't have to have bread," Noah assured her

in kinder tones than he had greeted her previous culinary disasters.

She snatched up a pot holder and dumped the whole ruined mess in the sink. "I just wanted for once to do something completely right."

"You've been doing plenty right."

"Oh, yes." Disgusted, she ran water over the bread. "I feel sure I am the champion of horse poop cleaners, feed spreaders and water trough cleaners."

"You also shine up a mean saddle," Noah commented, his tone dry.

She glared at him. "Stop making fun of me."

"I'm trying to tell you that you've been doing okay. You're coming along, Princess."

The hated nickname fueled her aggravation. "I know it must be amusing to you, watching me scurry around and struggle with the simplest things."

"I'm not laughing."

"You have to understand what it means to me to be doing any of this."

"Come on, Olivia, tell the truth. Is learning to cook spaghetti or muck out a stall really helping you decide what you want to do with your life?"

"I'm sure most people wouldn't understand, but it just feels good when I accomplish something on my own." She turned off the water and gazed ruefully at the soggy, black bread. "Maybe that's why screwing up something simple makes me so mad. It feels as if I'm reinforcing everything my father thinks about me."

Noah's tone was serious. "You don't have to stay here to prove anything to him. Someone of your background could get a job somewhere other than a horse farm."

"Doing what?" Olivia asked, looking up at him.

He rubbed his neck. "I don't know. Maybe you should call those friends you mentioned in Chicago, or some business associate of your father's who could lend you a hand. You could talk to them about what they could find for you."

She studied him in silence for a moment. "If I left you could hire someone competent to take my place, couldn't you?"

A line appeared between his eyebrows. "What are you talking about?"

"You could use what you're paying me to get someone who really knows what they're doing."

He made an impatient gesture. "This isn't about what I need, it's about you getting a suitable job."

"But you do need help, right?"

"Of course."

"My father has half as many horses as you do and twice as big a staff to care for them."

His expression tightened. "It's not the same thing. His stable is a collection that's mainly for pleasure, a rich man's trophy case. This is a business that has to turn a profit."

"If I had money, I'd invest in you."

He laughed shortly. "Thanks, but I'd settle for someone buying a yearling or two."

"I'd do that if I could."

The sweet concern and solid support in her voice touched Noah in an unexpected way. For some reason he felt like opening up to Olivia, and it was rare indeed for him to even consider discussing his business worries with anyone.

His mother had handed the reins of the farm to him when he was twenty-one, nearly twelve years ago. While she had her music lessons and a small retirement from the school system where she had taught after Owen nearly destroyed them, she also still needed an income from the farm. She trusted Noah to take care of things, and she didn't interfere. In turn, he didn't burden her.

Noah could talk to Jordan in a general sort of way, and he had a few friends in the business. But since Amy, there hadn't been anyone with whom he wanted to share the scope of his dreams or the limits of his checkbook.

Remembering how that turned out, he wondered why he felt like spilling his guts to Olivia. Maybe he was as lonely as he was horny, and she was simply here, a convenience. The very thought shamed him.

"We were talking about you," he said, bringing the conversation back in line. "About how maybe cleaning stables isn't really helping you."

"You were saying that, not me," Olivia retorted. "I'd like to hold on to this job until I've at least earned plane fare to reach my next destination, wherever that's going to be. If you'll remember, I've had some trouble with transporting myself and Puddin'."

"I could call around to some people I know, to find you a job somewhere in town," Noah suggested. He thought briefly about telling her he had talked to her father, that the man was wondering about her and might be softening. Then he reconsidered. "Middle Tennessee State University is in Murfreesboro. Surely there'd be something there for someone smart and industrious."

Her broad, beaming smile pulled him up short.

"What's wrong?"

"You called me smart and industrious."

"So?"

"Do you really think I'm smart?"

He couldn't resist teasing her. "You have figured out how to mix the feed, and you're coming right along with working the stove."

She replied by swatting him with a dish towel. "Very funny."

He continued, "Anyone who can clean up a leather bridle like you do should have no trouble landing an executive position."

"Stop it!" she ordered, and laughed as she swatted at him again.

Chuckling, Noah dodged the soggy towel and headed for the table. "Come on, Prin...I mean, Olivia." He grinned at her as he avoided the nickname she disliked so much. "I'll help you clean up."

"What happened to your 'you cook, you clean,' rule?"

"Rules can be broken, I guess," he said.

Olivia turned from picking charred, soggy bread out of the sink to gape at him. "I can't believe I'm hearing the inflexible Mr. Raybourne utter such blasphemy."

Her characterization of him sounded none too complimentary. "Inflexible?"

"You are a stickler for details."

"I just want things done right."

"And the right way is always your way."

"My way is generally the right way."

"You sound like my father," Olivia murmured as she dumped the mess in the trash can.

"Forgive me if I'm not flattered."

"It wasn't meant as a compliment."

Beside her at the sink, Noah set the plates on the counter. With her chin tilted at a challenging angle and brown eyes sparkling, she looked cute and sassy. Without thinking, he tweaked her impudent, upturned nose. "You're awfully flippant with your boss. I could fire you before you earn that flight money."

"You don't scare me."

"Really?" He leaned in closer, irresistibly drawn by her saucy grin. "And why is that?"

"If you were as mean as you want me to think you are, you never would have come back for me and Puddin' at that bus station."

He wondered what she would say if she knew it

had not been only kindness that had caused him to extend his help. More important, however, he wondered what she would do if he moved just a little bit closer, if he tasted that rosebud of a mouth she was lifting toward his.

"I'm not really so nice," he murmured, dismayed by the way desire roughened his voice.

Her eyes had gone all soft, the golden lights darkening. "I think you are nice. Very nice."

He kissed her then, before he could come to his senses. He kissed her, even as he was damning his foolishness to hell.

Chapter Seven

Olivia's fingers were cool and damp as she lifted them to touch Noah's cheek. The lips that opened beneath his own were hesitant at first. Then eager. Her willing and somehow innocent response took him from simple want to hardening need. There was no in between. No slow buildup. The speed rattled him so thoroughly that he backed away.

Holding her at arm's length, he fought to bring himself under control. She looked dazed, as if she wasn't quite sure of what had transpired between them.

"I'm sorry," he murmured.

"I'm not," she said.

"It was inappropriate for me to kiss you."

She stepped close to him once again and demanded, ''Why?''

''I'm your boss.''

''I won't sue.'' Her arms closed around his waist. ''I promise.''

Firmly Noah set her away from him again. ''This is crazy. I'm not going to take advantage of you this way.''

''I don't feel taken advantage of.''

''That's the worst part. You don't even realize how vulnerable you are.''

Her eyes narrowed. ''What does that mean?''

''You're in a rough place right now. Your whole life's been uprooted. You're looking for answers. It would be irresponsible of me to…'' He swallowed, thinking of just what he wanted to do. He drew in and released a long breath.

''What about what I want?''

''I'm not certain you know what you want.''

Brows drawing together, she took a step back. ''I hope you're not saying I can't think for myself, because—''

''No, of course not,'' Noah hurriedly assured her. ''I just don't think you're in a very good place to be making big decisions. Let's just chalk this up to an impetuous mistake.''

Hurt crept into her face. ''So you wish you hadn't kissed me?''

''No…I mean, yes…'' Frustrated, Noah rubbed his

chin. "What I'm trying to say is that it would be a mistake to act impulsively."

"Don't you ever get tired of being so in control?"

"I've found life works best that way."

She considered that with a frown, then shook her head. "I'm the last person to be lecturing on the way to conduct a life. I've never even had a life. But it seems to me things could get pretty darned dull if you left out the possibility of a surprise or two along the way."

"Surprises aren't always pleasant."

"But kissing you is," she replied. Before he could react, she pressed herself against him once again and twined her arms around his neck. "I don't really think you minded this surprise too much."

With a groan he gave in to her kiss, gave himself over to the pleasure of holding her close. Small but rounded, her body fit his in all the right places. He reached up and brushed one hand through the heavy, burnished curls at her neck, gently guiding her head back as their kiss deepened. He knew where they were headed. He knew all the reasons why they shouldn't. He had spelled them all out for her. But he was damned if he could stop himself. So much for Noah Raybourne's famous control. A red-haired princess had smashed it to pieces.

The sound of a car in the drive brought him back to earth.

"Damn," he muttered as a car door slammed. Puddin' went to the back door and barked.

"They'll go away," Olivia said, lifting her lips to his again.

"No." Noah could hear footsteps on the crushed pebble walkway near the kitchen. This was someone who knew him. Strangers would go to the front.

He stepped away from Olivia as his name was called from the back porch. "In here," he responded, frowning as he tried to place the deep, male tones. The screened porch door slapped shut, and a moment later Noah swung open the kitchen door to greet a tall, graying man clad in khakis and an expensive-looking cotton shirt.

"I hear you've got a prime yearling for sale," the man said, his voice booming as he held out his hand.

For a moment Noah couldn't believe his eyes. Finally, jaw squared, he clasped the outstretched hand. "Good evening, Jed."

The coolness of his tone drew Olivia's attention. This man clearly wasn't a friend.

But the older man evidently didn't detect Noah's reserve. He clapped him on the shoulder as he gave him a hearty handshake. "I know I should have called, but I was driving this way, and I remembered hearing about the yearling you're selling, and..." His words trailed away as his gaze widened to include Olivia. "I'm sorry. I'm interrupting your dinner—"

"We're finished with dinner," Noah said. He introduced Olivia to Jed Taylor, identifying him as the owner of a neighboring farm.

Jed backed toward the door. "Noah, I'll leave you

to your guest. I'll call you tomorrow and we'll see about talking some business.''

"Please stay," Olivia said. "I'm not really a guest.''

"Oh?" Interest sparked in the gaze the older man directed between her and Noah.

"Olivia works for me," Noah explained.

Jed lifted an eyebrow but made no further comment.

Noah gestured toward the door. "Let's go talk about my yearlings.'' He nodded to Olivia and turned to go.

She wanted him to indicate she would see him later. She knew she shouldn't expect anything more, but she did. After what had been happening between them when this man arrived, surely Noah could at least give her a smile. But he was all business, almost abrupt.

At the door the older man hesitated, rubbing his jaw. "There's one thing I probably should tell you, Noah.''

He turned in the doorway, frowning. "Yeah?''

"I'm buying for my daughter. For Amy.''

The name startled Olivia. *Amy? The same Amy who had jilted Noah?* Holding her breath, Olivia waited for a reaction from Noah.

His regard was stony. "A sale's a sale," he told Jed.

"I'm glad you see it that way," Jed replied. "There was a time—''

Noah cut him off, "Let's go look at my horses."

With a courteous goodbye to Olivia, Jed followed Noah out into the June dusk.

Through the window over the sink, Olivia watched them cross the yard and found herself filling with apprehension.

Noah's watch registered well after eleven before he turned out the lights in the office and headed for the house.

Jed Taylor had left several hours ago. Tomorrow he would send a trailer to pick up Cotton's Pride and another yearling to add to Amy's personal stable. Noah had started to ask if the horses were a wedding gift. He wasn't sure Jed would be that insensitive, but then again, Amy's father was one hard-nosed businessman. If Jed was looking for a deal on a horse he wanted, he wouldn't let a little matter like Amy having jilted Noah stand in his way.

Noah didn't care. At least he was sure the animal he had raised was going to a fine stable. Just as important, he could be certain Jed's check was good.

What did bother him was the sense that Jed thought he should be desperate enough to take his first, lowball offer. The man had seemed surprised when Noah was willing to walk away from the table rather than take less than what he wanted for his horses. Perhaps Jed's attitude really shouldn't have been such a shock to Noah. Three years ago, both Amy and her father thought he would jump at the chance to join his operation to theirs. Evidently, Jed hadn't learned much about Noah's determination.

And right now Noah didn't care. After Jed had departed, he had worked on his books, replanning his budget for the rest of the summer. The picture had become much rosier, even without Roger Franklin's money.

He crossed his screened porch, found the kitchen door unlocked and darted an irritated glance toward the darkened windows of Olivia's rooms. For someone who had spent most of her life living with high-tech security, she had a real problem with remembering locks.

But at least she was asleep. The paperwork he had done tonight could have waited. The real reason Noah had remained in his office was to avoid confronting what had happened between him and Olivia tonight. She had called their kisses a surprise. He knew they were a mistake. Seeing Jed, and being reminded of Amy, had simply reinforced what Noah knew to be the truth—he was better off avoiding princesses.

A bark greeted him just inside the kitchen, and Puddin' padded in from the hall. Scowling, Noah followed the dog and found her mistress asleep on his den sofa in front of a muted television set. She was resting so deeply she didn't even stir when he and Puddin' came in the room.

He thought briefly of covering her with an afghan and leaving her here. But that wasn't the signal he wanted to send. So he leaned over and shook her shoulder.

She came slowly awake, blinking and stretching, then smiling up at him with a lazy sweetness that could have roped Noah in if he let it.

He backed away. "You should be in bed."

Raking her hair from her face, she said, "I waited for you to come home."

Noah switched off the television set. "It's really late."

"Did Amy's father buy Cotton's Pride?"

So Jed's identity hadn't been lost on Olivia. Noah nodded. "He took two yearlings."

Olivia studied him for a moment. "That's good, isn't it?"

"Of course."

"Even though it's Amy's father who's buying."

"His money is as green as the next guy's."

She studied him for a moment. "Then what's wrong?"

"It's late. Time we were both asleep."

"But you're angry about something."

"I just want to go to bed."

"Did it bother you to see Mr. Taylor?"

"Of course not. I've known Jed Taylor my whole life."

"So you knew Amy your whole life, too."

Patience at an end, Noah said, "Would you stop with the twenty questions? I'm tired."

"And you want to get rid of me."

He decided honesty couldn't hurt. "Yeah, I do. Go to bed, and leave me alone."

She pushed herself to her feet. "I really don't understand why selling those horses to Mr. Taylor has made you angry with me."

Noah simply avoided her gaze. "Just quit inventing melodramas and go to bed, Princess."

She bit her lip, looking hurt and confused. "I don't understand you. I mean, I thought we…connected."

"We kissed," Noah replied flatly. "Just a kiss, Olivia."

"Several kisses," she corrected.

"All of which were stupid on my part."

"I don't think you really believe that."

Noah stooped, picked up Puddin' and placed her in Olivia's arms. "Take your dog and go to your room."

The order made Olivia feel about an inch tall. "Noah—"

He cut her off with an angry wave of his hand. "I don't feel like arguing about something that doesn't matter anyway. Lock the door behind you on the way out."

Something that doesn't matter. His dismissal of their kisses left Olivia with no choice but to leave. Seething, she marched across the yard to her small, shabby rooms above the garage. She was so tired she ought to drop right off to sleep, but instead all she did was pace.

Eventually her anger gave way to self-doubt. She had done something wrong again. Something that put

him off. Maybe she had been too bold. Or too nice.
For goodness sake, she didn't know anything about
flirting or romance. How was she supposed to act?
She had been certain he was as affected by kissing
her as she was by kissing him. So why did he insist
their kiss didn't matter to him? In her inexperience
she had clearly screwed up the whole moment. What
did a man like Noah want from a woman?

Olivia decided she needed some advice. Unfortunately the only person she could turn to also happened
to be Noah's mother. That might be a problem, except
that Carmen was one exceptionally cool mom. She
might even be on Olivia's side.

Carmen's house was at the opposite end of the farm
from Noah's, set on a gentle rise and framed by a tall
stand of trees. Lush shrubbery and disciplined flower
beds bordered the small, whitewashed structure, while
wildflowers grew in seemingly unplanned abandon
about the perimeter of the smooth, green yard. A vegetable garden lay to the south. Among the well-tended
rows of plants was where Olivia spied Noah's mother
the following evening.

The older woman called out and waved a gloved
hand. Despite the heat, she also wore a long-sleeved
shirt and a hat to discourage insect bites. "I was just
wishing for company."

"You're busy," Olivia observed. "I don't want to
interrupt."

"I'm just piddling," Carmen assured her as she

straightened from the plant she had tied to a stake with what appeared to be a pair of panty hose. "Isn't it lovely that there's a purpose for all the hose we women ruin?"

Olivia agreed. "Why do you tie the plants up?"

"So they'll stand straight in the rain and the sun and hold up when the tomatoes start to weigh them down. Soon we'll have some red, ripe tomatoes for our salads."

"Sounds delicious."

"The beans are coming in now." Carmen nodded to the half-filled basket she had left at the end of a row. "And the squash. As usual I've got more zucchini than four families could eat. I was just going to go in and make some zucchini corn bread that Noah especially likes."

"Would you show me how?" Olivia asked.

"Come in the house where it's cool. Tell me how dinner went last night." From Carmen's slow, knowing smile, Olivia realized that Noah's mother had indeed figured out that last night's dinner had been more than a cooking exercise. Of course, with Olivia running around agonizing over pasta and tablecloths and checking her reflection in the mirror every other second, Carmen would have had to be blind not to see what was up.

Still, Olivia flushed under the woman's regard. "I can see you know that I…umm…like Noah."

"My dear, I figured that out right from the start."

Olivia did a double take. "But I didn't know it then."

"Mothers can sense these things," Carmen assured her, leading the way down the row of vegetables. She flashed Olivia another conspiratorial smile. "I also know that Noah's pretty interested in you, too."

"How can you tell?"

"Well, for starters, he won't talk about you. He doesn't want to give me any ideas about you two, so he pretty much changes the subject every time your name comes up." Reaching the edge of the garden, the older woman stripped off her gloves and hat. "Now tell me about last night."

Bending to pick up the basket, Olivia sighed. "I burned the bread, but things went fine." Remembering the way Noah had kissed her, she sighed again. "Better than fine, actually."

As they turned along the path to the house, Carmen's grin was downright girlish. "If things went fine, then why do I sense there's something wrong?"

"After Mr. Taylor came—"

"Taylor?" Carmen stopped dead in her tracks. "Jed Taylor came to see Noah?"

"Amy's father. He bought two yearlings."

Blinking in surprise, Carmen said, "They live not five miles away, but to my knowledge, Noah hasn't spoken to one of the Taylors since the wedding fell through." She shook her head. "You say Noah sold Jed Taylor horses?"

"For Amy."

"Well, well…that's very interesting." Carmen pursed her lips as she headed for the house.

She took Olivia in the back way, across a shallow porch where she deposited the basket of produce. Olivia followed Carmen's example and left her shoes by the door before entering the kitchen. The floor tiles were cool against her feet, and the aromas that hung in air made her mouth water.

"What smells so wonderful?"

Carmen placed the zucchini she carried in the sink. "Just soup. Haven't you eaten?"

After a day in which Noah seemed intent on avoiding Olivia as much as possible, he had taken off somewhere just before dinner, advising her only to "fend for herself." She had grabbed a most unsatisfying sandwich and left Puddin' at the house before heading to Carmen's.

"Sit down," Carmen instructed, gesturing to the round oak table tucked in the kitchen corner.

Moments later, Olivia was savoring a spicy vegetable soup and a hunk of homemade wheat bread. The flavors fairly exploded on her tongue. "I want to know how to do this," she told the older woman. "I want to be able to make something so simple taste this great."

"Cooking is easy if you want to learn."

"I really do want to," Olivia said, surprised by how much she meant it. She enjoyed another spoonful of soup before asking, "Was Amy much of a cook?"

Carmen laughed as she took the chair next to Olivia's. "Amy was better at ordering from a menu."

Olivia could certainly identify with that. "Did Noah care?"

"Noah thought that was one of those things that would magically work out after they got married. He thought that about a lot of things that had to do with Amy."

"Because he loved her?"

Carmen looked thoughtful as she broke off a piece of bread for herself. "I don't know that it was about love. In my opinion Noah simply assumed what Amy intended to do about any number of things. He didn't listen very well to what she wanted or needed."

"Hadn't he known her for a long time?"

"We knew the Taylors, mainly because Jed owns a farm. It's a first-class operation, but Jed has family money, and he's certainly not dependent on his horses for a living."

"Like my father," Olivia murmured.

"The Taylors moved in a different world from us. Amy went to a private school in Nashville. She was horse crazy, so she spent a fair amount of time at the farm. However, she spent a lot of vacations skiing or at the beach."

"So how did she and Noah get together?"

"Well, they'd always known each other, through horse shows and such, but she's five or six years younger. She really got into the operation of her father's farm after she got out of college. One day she and Noah were at a breeder's meeting. They started talking, and that was that.''

"Until she stood him up at the altar.''

Carmen sighed. "I would never say this to Noah, because he was destroyed, but Amy did him a favor. They didn't want the same things out of life.''

"They must have thought so at one time.''

"Until Amy realized Noah really wouldn't go along with her plan to sell out to her father.''

Olivia was aghast. "He would never do that. This farm is like one of his arms or legs.''

Softly Carmen said, "It's interesting that you already know that much about Noah, after just a few weeks here. Amy never figured it out.''

"So she jilted him.''

"Imagine how it rattles Noah to realize he's interested in someone with a background similar to Amy's.''

"I'm not her,'' Olivia protested. "He and I met because I was trying to get away from my father's control and my useless life.''

"You were also running away from your wedding.''

Propping an elbow on the table, Olivia sighed. "Considering all that Amy and I have in common, it's a wonder Noah ever brought me here.''

"And perhaps that's why he did,'' Carmen said, a thoughtful look on her face. "Having you here has probably helped him work through some leftover hostility toward her.''

"Forgive me if I'm not thrilled about being used," Olivia retorted. Then an awful truth struck her.

Wasn't *using* exactly what she had done with Noah?

First she used him to sneak away. Then she accepted the job he offered in order to prove something to her father. She hadn't paused to consider whether there really was a job, or if Noah could even afford to pay her. She had simply used his generosity as a lifeline to pull herself out of the mire she had made out of her escape from her wedding and her father's control.

But sometime during the past few weeks, Noah had ceased to be simply a means to an end. He no longer represented an escape. He wasn't just her boss. He was a man. An intense, loyal man who worked long and hard to keep what was his. From what she knew about his background—his stepfather's shortcomings and his half sister's disability and death—he had seen a lot of trouble. Yet he had emerged a fair, honest and decent man. A man of principles. Olivia had come to admire and respect him. She wanted him to feel the same way about her.

She looked at Carmen. "I came over here this evening to ask for some advice about attracting Noah's attention."

The older woman laid a hand on Olivia's arm. "You have his attention, my dear. Most definitely."

"But I was looking for some tips on feminine wiles," Olivia admitted with a rueful smile. "I think

I wanted to trick Noah into acting on his feelings.'' She held up a hand before Carmen could reply. ''But I don't really think I need those tips now.''

''Why?''

''Because I don't want to trick Noah. I don't want to play games with him.''

Carmen eased back in her chair, listening.

''I don't know anything about flirting,'' Olivia continued. ''My father kept my interactions with the opposite sex to a minimum. Besides being afraid of my being snatched by some lunatic, he also feared I'd fall prey to a fortune hunter. By the time I got out of college, he had me convinced I couldn't trust my own judgment about what street to walk down, much less what man to date. Because of all that I don't really know who I am. So why should I start playacting some part to get anyone's attention?''

''I think you know more about yourself than you think,'' Carmen observed, a pleased smile curving her lips.

Olivia brushed a tendril of hair off her cheek. ''No, I don't. Most of the time I'm pretty confused, except about—'' She broke off, flushing over what she had been about to confess.

''What?'' Carmen prompted.

Taking a deep breath, Olivia said, ''There is one thing I'm not confused about. Your son is a really special man. I'm sure of that much.'' Cheeks burning, she met Carmen's gaze.

The older woman got up and gave her a hug. "Yes, he is, my dear. And if I could offer some advice…"

"Of course."

"You're right to realize Noah doesn't respond to games. So just be yourself. See what develops."

With a rueful chuckle, Olivia said, "As I told you, I'm not even sure who I am, so that won't be easy."

Carmen gave her shoulders another squeeze. "I'm telling you to trust your instincts. I have a feeling they're right on target."

"I hope so," Olivia murmured. She tipped her head back to look at Carmen. "Thanks for listening."

"Anytime." After one last hug, Carmen headed for the sink. "Now, are you going to help me with this zucchini, or what? We can talk over some plans for the day camp while we work."

Olivia got to her feet, eager to be busy. Her stated purpose for leaving her father's house and ending up here had been to discover the possibilities of life. Being free to choose to spend this evening with this kind and special woman was only one of the pleasures she had discovered. Making something out of these long, green vegetables Carmen had grown herself might well be another. Each and every day she was finding that it was the simple things that brought her the biggest rewards in terms of happiness.

Later Olivia walked through the humid night, clutching a foil-wrapped plate of zucchini corn bread she had baked with only supervision from Carmen. She hummed, happy for no real reason. Even Noah's scowl as he met her at his kitchen door didn't bring her down.

"This is for you." She handed him the plate before stooping to pick up Puddin' and give Mrs. Whiskers a scratch behind the ears.

Noah was still frowning when she straightened. "I didn't know where you were."

"You must have missed my note." Olivia nodded toward the message she had left on the table.

His frown darkened.

She smiled against her pet's silky fur, then settled her features before looking up at Noah again. "Beginning tomorrow, your mother will be needing my help to start getting ready for the camp. Is that going to be okay?"

His grunt could have been a yes or a no. "Are you sure you know what you're getting into?"

"No," she retorted with a laugh. "But that's just fine. I'm open to just about anything."

Eyes narrowing, Noah regarded her for a moment. "Is there something wrong? Did you and Mom hit the cooking sherry?"

Instead of honoring that foolish question with any sort of reply, Olivia stifled a yawn. "I'm going to bed. See you in the morning."

She left Noah staring after her with a bemused expression. Which was just fine, she decided. The instincts Carmen had urged her to trust were telling Olivia that she had been spending altogether too much time courting Noah's favor and worrying what he thought about her. Discovering exactly who she was and what she thought about herself was more important right now.

She knew she was something more than the "princess" Noah thought her to be. More than a spoiled rich brat or a bride on the run. She was someone altogether different from the Amy Taylor who had left him standing at the altar. Maybe someday Noah would realize that, as well.

"A girl can dream," she whispered to Puddin' as they climbed the stairs beside the garage.

Chapter Eight

Noah had lived his entire life on this farm. He knew the contour of the land as well as he knew the planes of his own face. The woods that rimmed the green pastures, the creek that bisected the northeast corner, the dip in the drive where it branched between house and outbuildings. Unprepossessing as it was, this was his home. Shaded by memories. Brightened by his hopes and dreams. There was no other place he had ever thought of living.

Nevertheless, when he was eighteen, his mother had insisted he broaden his horizons, at least a little. He'd enrolled at nearby Middle Tennessee State University. The experience had been good. His mind had opened to new possibilities, and he met people from a multitude of backgrounds. He was justifiably proud of the degree he had worked so hard to obtain. Yet he still chose to live here, to do the work he had decided he loved when he was just a child.

On this farm, in the life he lived, in the work that he accomplished, Noah found a fulfillment he didn't expect most people to understand.

So why did Olivia seem to be enjoying herself here? Thriving, even? Noah could not decide what was up with this rich girl turned Raybourne Farms' all-purpose employee.

Over a week had passed since he let down his guard and foolishly kissed her. He hadn't known what to expect her to do after he rejected her. Leave, maybe. Or perhaps throw a temperamental fit worthy of a spoiled princess. Instead she had thrown herself into the workaday life of the farm with a renewed enthusiasm that both intrigued and annoyed Noah.

Living and working as they did, he couldn't avoid her. Lord knows he had tried, but she was at hand wherever he turned. She had taken to rising at dawn and starting breakfast. Tuesday morning she attempted pancakes—a little too thick, but still not bad. The next day she prepared a vegetable lasagna that he had reluctantly called wonderful, to her delight.

Learning to cook had become a crusade of sorts, an interest that seemed strange for a young woman used to a gourmet chef. Noah was unsure what to make of her pleasure over a success in the kitchen. Was it some kind of put on? Last night he had found her poring over the cookbooks she had unearthed from a kitchen cabinet. She was planning to cook Sunday dinner tomorrow for him, Jordan and Carmen.

Cooking wasn't all that absorbed her time. She still attended to a multitude of menial tasks in the barn. She worked under Jordan's tutelage training two fillies and with Noah's mother on preparations for the upcoming camp. She had painted her rooms a sunshine yellow. She had even goaded Noah into teaching her to play chess. He had agreed, reluctantly, and now spent a tortured hour every other night seated across from her in his den. Apparently she really wanted to learn.

He just wanted her.

His desire for her was out of control. Last Sunday, when she could have been resting, he had found her in his mother's garden, filling a sketch pad with tomato plants. When he asked her why, she had called the ripening, red globes ''beautiful.'' Noah had been torn between suggesting she had been out in the sun too long, and simply taking her into his arms and capturing her smile beneath his kiss. He had concocted quite a little fantasy about the two of them among the tassel-topped rows of corn, making love in the rich, dark soil with the sunshine hot on their skin.

She had infected him. He was sick with yearning for her. He had never felt this way about anyone, not even Amy.

Hell, at this very moment he should be in the office

working up a stud contract. Instead, he was piddling around with repairs to a loose plank on a fence and watching Olivia with Cody up at the old supply shed his mother had commandeered years ago for her camp headquarters.

Unless Noah was seeing things, Olivia had somehow talked Cody into trying on one of the costumes Carmen had borrowed from her old school. Noah had heard the two women discussing putting on some sort of production for the kids. It looked as if Cody was now some kind of...squirrel?

"Hey, chief, what's up?"

Jordan's hearty greeting and clap on the shoulder distracted Noah from his study of Olivia and Cody. He returned to hammering the loose plank into place. "I'm just trying to keep the place from falling in," he groused to the older man. "I told Cody to do this."

"But the fair Livvie took the boy's attention." Jordan chuckled. "You shouldn't blame the boy. It appeared to me that you were more interested in her than the fence post, too."

Noah grunted a noncommittal reply as he pulled on the plank to test its soundness.

The older man leaned his elbows on the fence and gazed toward the shed with appreciation. "She is a looker, isn't she?"

"If you like the type."

"And you do," Jordan said with another crusty laugh.

The protest Noah started died under his trainer's

knowing regard. With a sigh he braced himself against the fence and looked with unabashed longing toward Olivia. Her throaty laughter floated across the field and washed over him like a caress. ''I'm a fool,'' he told Jordan. ''I know better than to fall for a woman like her.''

''And just what sort is she?''

''A rich man's daughter.''

''She didn't choose her parents.''

''But it means she's not really interested in the likes of me.''

''If you believe that, you've not been paying attention.''

Noah hooked his hammer in his tool belt and shared the most likely theory he had come up with about the way Olivia had been acting. ''If she's interested at all it's because I'm a novelty. The farm's a novelty, too. A game she's playing to pass the time.''

''Don't be so sure about that.''

''I'm not really up for being some spoiled brat's plaything. I've been there and done that.''

''I think you're selling our Livvie short.'' Jordan paused to release a stream of tobacco juice. ''If she were anything like that fancy piece you got yourself mixed up with before, she would have hightailed it out of here that first morning.''

''This is all some big adventure for her. She'll be ready to leave soon enough.''

''Why're you so sure?''

"Because I just know," Noah said, irritation creeping into his tone. "I know her type. I know what she really wants. I know just what will happen if I get any more involved with her than I already am."

Rheumy eyes narrowing, Jordan regarded him with a frown. "Must be nice to know so awful damn much about what everybody else thinks."

"It doesn't take smarts or talent to predict what's going to happen with Olivia Franklin. Her father's one of the wealthiest men in the country. It stands to reason she's going to get tired of the joys we can offer her here." His tone was heavy with sarcasm.

"If all that money made her so happy, why'd she run away from it?"

Noah brushed that aside with a sweep of his hand. "Temporary insanity."

"About a month of it so far," Jordan observed wryly. As laughter spilled from the shed once again, he grinned. "Sure sounds to me like she's miserable."

Noah backed away from the fence. "I've got too much to do to be wasting my time on this." He turned and started for the barn.

"Maybe one day you'll wish you'd wasted a little more."

The older man's gruff comment drew Noah back around. "What's that?"

"Right now you've got all the time you can waste," Jordan snarled. "But in the blink of an eye, it'll be gone, and what'll you have to show for it?"

Noah was startled by the trainer's obvious anger.

Jordan shook a finger at him. "Someday, sooner than you think, you'll be an old man, Noah Raybourne. Are you going to be looking back with regrets? Will you wish you had at least taken a chance on that redhead over there?"

"But I know—"

"Oh, yes, you *know* so much." Jordan spat his plug of tobacco on the ground and glared at Noah. "I think what you really know about that pretty, pretty girl up there could fit on the head of a pin. And you know even less about yourself."

Before Noah could protest, the trainer continued, "Don't be looking all pop-eyed at me, boy. You're acting like an ass about Livvie because of that little tart who left you at the altar. In my opinion you were well rid of Amy Taylor. But mark my words, you'll rue the day you sat on your hands and let Livvie walk away from here."

Too stunned to make a reply, Noah stood unmoving while the older man jammed his cap on his head and stalked away. A few moments later Noah heard the engine in the man's pickup spring to life. The truck pulled away from the stables and headed down the driveway. To Noah's knowledge, it was the first time in years his trainer had left the place while there was still work to be done.

Jordan Camp had come to work on this farm when Noah was less than a year old. He'd remained after Noah's father died, stayed until Owen drove him away. He came back when Noah and Carmen needed him. The old man had paddled Noah's behind, poured him his first shot of whisky, held him in his arms the night Charly died. Yet Noah had never seen him as angry as he was right now. All over "Livvie."

Damn. Had the princess enchanted them all?

Staring toward the shed, where his mother was now standing with Olivia, and Cody was still scampering around in ninety-degree heat in some sort of squirrel costume, Noah could only conclude that the answer was yes. Olivia had cast a spell over all of Raybourne Farm. Most especially over him.

How long was he going to fight it?

He answered his own question by climbing over the fence and striding toward the shed. Did he imagine it, or did Olivia's smile spread even wider than usual as he approached the open-ended, weathered board building. Noah found himself hoping so. For once, he didn't fight the feeling.

Returning her grin, he nodded toward Cody's furry outfit. "What have you done with my stable hand?"

"I just had to see this on someone," Olivia replied. "Your mother and I have written a little skit for the opening of the camp, and I wanted to make sure this outfit looked cuddly, not scary."

"Well, Cody looks right cuddly to me," Noah drawled as he unhooked his tool belt and set it on a long, wooden table. "I'm glad he could help."

Cody snatched off the squirrel head. "I'm sorry, boss. I know I should be working on those repairs you gave me to do, but Olivia and Miss Carmen asked—''

Noah waved off the boy's explanations. "Don't worry. I'm sure Olivia and my mother were most persuasive."

''I'll get right to work,'' Cody continued, red-faced and huffing as he struggled with the suit.

Carmen tugged the squirrel mitts off his hands. "There's no need to get yourself in a lather."

''No, he'd better hurry.'' Noah's gruff tone earned him a glare from his mother and a puzzled look from Olivia. He suppressed a grin.

''Sure thing, boss,'' Cody muttered, color deepening even more.

''I want you to get busy,'' Noah continued. Then he grinned. ''Take the rest of the afternoon off. Call your friends. Go swimming. Have a good Saturday night.''

Cody gaped at him. "But, boss, I need—"

''To take the rest of the day off with pay.'' Noah patted the boy's fur-clad shoulder. ''After wearing this suit in this heat, you deserve combat pay.''

Chuckling, Olivia finished undoing the opening down the back of the suit. ''Cody, if I were you, I'd get out of here before Noah comes to his senses.''

With a grin the teenager stepped free of the costume.

Carmen said, ''I'm going to town for some shopping and dinner with a friend. I'll give you a ride home, Cody.''

As the pair headed toward Carmen's house, Olivia turned to Noah with a smile. "That was a nice thing to do. He works so hard."

"He's a good boy."

"He thinks you hung the moon."

Noah stooped to pick up the discarded squirrel head and scowled at the painted-on smile. "Are you sure this thing won't terrify the kids?"

"Let's hope not." Olivia folded the rest of the costume and led the way deeper into the shed.

She had learned from Carmen that the building was nearly as old as the farm. The gray-planked walls and heavy, wooden beams had been set in place by Noah's grandfather. After being replaced by a more-modern equipment shed closer to the stables, the space had been used mainly for storage of odds and ends until Carmen claimed it for the camp. An addition had been added to the rear, while the original structure had been made weathertight, floored and wired for electricity. The opening at one end had been replaced by two large, metal garage doors. With these rolled up, the windows open and the four ceiling fans whirling above, the shed was a perfect place for rainy-day camp activities.

Even in today's heat Olivia found it comfortable. "These big, old shade trees keep this place cool," she commented to Noah.

"Just wait until it's pouring rain and the place is filled with twenty or thirty kids. It'll get plenty warm in here."

Olivia placed the folded squirrel suit in a large, black trunk. "I know it will be busy, but I can't wait for camp to get started. Your mother is so excited."

"It's the highlight of her year." Noah stowed the squirrel head away and closed the trunk's lid. "But it will be a madhouse around here for two weeks."

"Do you mind at all?"

"When it gets crazy, I just remind myself of Charly and how much she loved being outside with the horses. The camp keeps her memory alive."

Surprised and pleased to find Noah in such an open and friendly mood, Olivia sat down on the trunk. She risked a personal question. "Neither you or your mother really say much about Charly. What was she like?"

Though she half expected him to make some evasive reply, Noah's features softened. "You wouldn't expect a kid with all her problems to laugh so much. But she did. Even when she was really small, I'd push her outside, and she'd hold her face up to the sun and just giggle, like she was so happy to be alive."

"Sounds as if you were a doting big brother," Olivia observed softly.

"I can't imagine why anyone wouldn't love her." Noah's face tightened. "I never understood why Owen didn't."

"Oh, but surely he loved her," Olivia protested.

"You'd never have known it by the way he acted."

"The way Carmen explains things, he simply couldn't get past her limitations."

"He couldn't get past his own limitations."

"Maybe he felt guilty for some reason, as if her problems were his fault."

Noah met Olivia's gaze straight on. "I guess I don't want to make excuses for him."

"I certainly understand that." Olivia sighed. "I can't compare my father to your stepfather, but it's easier to stay angry with him when I don't make excuses."

"So you're angry with him still?"

"Maybe disappointed is a better description." She crossed her legs on the top of the trunk and rested her elbows on her denim-clad knees. "In his efforts to protect me, my father robbed me of the chance to grow. He took so much from me."

"He also gave you so much. You had a beautiful home, an expensive education, travel—"

"And absolutely no choice about anything to do with my life," Olivia retorted. "He doesn't respect me enough to think I can make a choice. You heard what he thinks of me..." Her voice caught in her throat, but she fought past the emotion. "It's going to take a long time to forgive him for that. Sometimes I'm not sure I can."

"But you're thinking about forgiveness. I don't even associate the word with Owen."

Olivia tipped her head back to study Noah's stony expression. "Did you ever resent your mother for marrying him?"

"Of course. Just before he left, when he was selling

everything out from under us, I thought I hated her. I was sixteen, an age where you can stay angry, especially at your parents, for a long, long time.''

''And how did you get past it?''

''She kept showing up, you know. She didn't give up on this farm, which I loved. It would have been easy for her to sell out and move away from here, but she stayed. She was determined to save this place for me.''

''I can imagine she was frightened.''

Noah eased down on the trunk beside her. ''Looking back now, I think she was just relieved to have Owen out of our lives. Making that decision made her strong. She worked like a madwoman for years. Got up every morning with the sun and did chores before me or Charly were awake. She got all of us, including herself, off to school, taught all day, then came home and worked beside me and Jordan every afternoon and evening. The only time I saw her falter was when Charly died.''

''Was that completely unexpected?'' Olivia asked softly.

He shook his head. ''Charly was so fragile, no one thought she would make it past two or three. But she fooled them all. She was a fighter. The winter she was eleven she came down with a simple cold. But before we knew it she had pneumonia. The doctors tried everything, but her lungs wouldn't clear. She died here at home with Mom and me and Jordan.''

It seemed very natural for Olivia to reach out and

clasp Noah's hand. Instead of resisting, as she expected he might, he folded his fingers around hers. "I'm so sorry," she said.

In reply Noah lifted his free hand and touched her cheek. The air around them felt suddenly very warm and heavy, as if the fans whirling above their heads were moving in slow motion. Olivia thought she could hear her own heart beating as Noah leaned forward and kissed her.

"I know I shouldn't do this," he whispered as he drew away.

"Then why do it?"

"Because wanting to touch you is eating me alive." The confession came with a scowl.

The distinctly unlover-like assertion made Olivia pull back, tugging her hand free and sliding off the trunk. "You certainly don't look very pleased about the situation."

"I'd give just about anything if I weren't feeling this way about you."

"Exactly how is that?"

"Like I need to know everything about you." His blue eyes steady on hers, his voice deepened. "How you'd move if we made love. What you would say. How I would need to touch you to make you respond."

She was responding without even a touch, her limbs heavy, her breath quickening, a languid heat at the juncture of her thighs. She didn't resist when Noah reached out and pulled her forward, so that she stood between his outstretched legs. She didn't protest when he kissed her again. Or when his hands drifted down her body, lingering over the swell of her breasts, then cupping her behind and drawing her tight against him.

With a soft, muffled groan, she gave herself over to his touch. To his mouth, whose gentle demands became more insistent. To her own excitement, which drew her in so quickly. Almost immediately, just kissing Noah didn't feel like enough. Just touching him wasn't enough. Her passion urged her on, while her inexperience left her uncertain of what she really wanted or what she should ask of him.

Noah seemed to have no such problems. He tugged her shirt free of her jeans, then his hands were warm against her bare skin. Drawing back, his gaze steady on hers, he undid each button of her shirt. She didn't think about resisting but also couldn't seem to help him.

Heat suffused her whole body when he pushed her shirt open. Breathing hard, she closed her eyes as his fingertips traced the upper edge of her bra where her breasts swelled against the lace. He stroked up her cleavage, then down once again. The astonishing pleasure made her nipples pucker in response. Then moist, gentle pressure pulled at one of the ripening buds.

Olivia's eyes flew open. Her knees almost buckled as Noah's mouth laved first one breast, then the other through the lace of her bra. No one, not even Marshall, had ever touched her this way.

"You're gorgeous," Noah whispered as he dipped his head to taste the skin of her bare midriff.

"No," she protested, steadying herself with her hands on his shoulders.

"Perfect," he murmured.

"Too short," she gasped.

Instead of answering, his lips wandered back to her breasts.

"And too round."

Noah looked up at her. "I like curves."

"But—"

"Women are supposed to have curves." With one, quick movement, he undid the front clasp of her bra.

Olivia's whole body flushed scarlet as her full, round breasts fell free. She jerked with pleasure when Noah cupped her in his hands. His mouth against her bare nipple made her whimper and gasp his name.

Pressing his face to her throat, he groaned. "I want you."

"And I want you." Her voice was shaking, but her intent was steady as she pressed one leg intimately close to his crotch.

He groaned again. "Move like that again and I may explode."

She responded with another wiggle against the bulge between his legs.

He grasped her hips and held them steady. "Don't do that, Olivia. Just hold on."

"But—"

"Just hold on," he whispered again as his arms encircled and held her close. Olivia could feel his heart pounding in his chest, a rhythm matched by the frantic pace of her own pulse.

Noah's voice was low against her ear. "Let's slow down a minute."

Taking it slow was the last thing on Olivia's mind. "But—"

"I don't want it like this," he murmured. "Not here. Not with you."

Frustration warred with delight inside her. That he clearly wanted this moment to be special was touching. Yet every pulse point still yearned for his touch. Her body was as primed and ready as his. Why should they wait? Why did he get to choose?

"I want you, Noah." She pressed her lips against the side of his neck, then trailed kisses across the faint stubble of his jaw. "I want you now."

"And the princess always gets what she wants?" His teasing tone took the sting out of the hated nickname.

"Noah, please..." Her lips closed over his.

Her soft entreaty and gentle kiss were almost Noah's undoing. Yet he held back. He wanted her with a ferocity close to desperation. It felt as if he had been wanting her forever. But this wasn't the right place. She deserved candlelight. Wine. Soft sheets. Romance. He summoned all his self-control, set her away from him and stood.

Modestly holding her blouse together, Olivia blinked at him in surprise.

"I think we should back up a step or two." He cleared his throat. "Let's...go somewhere."

"Go?"

"You know, dinner and a movie."

"Noah, I don't—"

"Let's get away for a few hours."

She was looking at him as if he had sprouted a second head. "You've hardly left the place since you got here," he continued. "Let's get in the truck, go somewhere and clear our heads."

"And what if I don't want my head cleared?"

"Olivia, let's just...go." Not waiting for her reaction, Noah turned and headed outside. "Be ready at six."

He wasn't certain about his reasoning. Maybe he thought that by leaving he would come to his senses. Maybe he thought she would come to hers. All he knew for certain was that it felt wrong to simply take her in the dusty surroundings of this supply shed. Now that he had committed himself to pursuing some sort of relationship with her, he wanted it to be the right way. *His* way.

Exactly at six Noah appeared at the bottom of the stairs leading to Olivia's rooms. Though she was ready and watching for him, she poked her head out the door and told him she needed a few more minutes. She told herself she wasn't playing games, but she experienced a perverse sense of power at knowing he was pacing outside. He had wanted to wait, so now he could wait.

Puddin's bark seemed to hold a note of disapproval as Olivia took another peek at herself in the bathroom mirror. She ignored the dog and ran her fingers through her hair one more time. There wasn't much she could do with her humidity-challenged curls. Nor could she do anything about her wardrobe. Her only choice was her latest discount store purchase of a moss-green, sleeveless sweater and matching full, patterned skirt. At least it was a change from the jeans she wore day in and day out.

She took a deep breath and released it slowly. How were she and Noah supposed to eat in a public place or sit quietly in a darkened theater with what had happened between them earlier simmering just beneath the surface?

"This is going to be torture," she told Puddin' before opening the door.

But from the moment Olivia looked down the stairs and her gaze met Noah's, she felt anything but tortured.

A slow smile of appreciation spread across his face as she walked down the steps to meet him. He took her hand and brought it to his lips. "You look incredible."

She flushed under his approval. "It's the outfit. Better than ripped jeans, huh?"

"No, it's you." He dipped his head and kissed her. "Come on, Princess, your carriage awaits."

Instead of resenting the nickname, she realized it fit. She did feel a little like Cinderella. Enchantment was in the air.

They drove west of Nashville, to the town of Franklin. In a cozy, brick-walled restaurant, they ate a delicious, candlelit dinner. Olivia lingered over her chicken-and-artichoke entree, and insisted on tasting the mushroom sauce with Noah's veal chops. He laughed as she dug through her purse in search of pen and paper in which to record details and perhaps incorporate the ingredients in an upcoming meal.

Afterward they decided to forgo the movie in favor of a stroll in the warm, summer air. The town was charming, with bricked streets and sidewalks, flowers spilling from baskets and planters and one fascinating shop window after another filled with antiques and decorative items. Down the side streets they glimpsed Civil War era homes restored to their former glory and now used as residences, offices, bed and breakfast inns and shops.

In particular, Olivia's interest was captivated by a shop showcasing fine stained glass work by local artisans. One large panel featured a sunflower design that she simply loved. She could just imagine the light beaming through the intricately joined colored panels. The work was so good that even at several hundred dollars, Olivia knew it was a steal. But the price was still much more than she could afford.

She stood in front of it for a long time, looking at the price tag, then sighing as she turned away. She found Noah watching her.

"You thinking of buying?" he asked.

"It would look perfect in the window in my room," she replied with a shrug. "But it's not something I need."

Noah studied the price tag for a moment, a frown collecting on his brow.

Detecting an unwelcome shift in his mood, Olivia laughed and tugged on his arm. "Come on, let's check out that shop next door before it's closing time."

She led him out on the street and from store window to store window, gradually cajoling him back into a good mood. In front of a display of Civil War memorabilia, she turned to him with a smile. "Do you know this is my first real date?"

Noah laughed. "I am quite sure Marshall sprang for dinner and a movie every once in a while."

"Of course he did. But one of my father's 'suits' was always with us. It's hard to think of a group outing as a real date."

"I don't think I would have liked that," Noah murmured, then leaned forward to kiss her. "Having some goon looking over your shoulder every moment must have been strange, from a romantic point of view."

"From every point of view. I hated it," Olivia admitted. Then she laughed. "For a long time I couldn't even admit to myself that I hated it. It was easier just to pretend it was okay. I told myself that being watched made me feel safe and protected. In reality it made me feel stupid.''

"Stupid?''

"Like I couldn't take care of myself.''

"After all that time of being protected and followed, how do you feel now? Safe?''

She looked left and right, studying the couples and families who were also enjoying the beautiful summer evening. "I feel safe with you.'' Facing Noah, Olivia reached out and threaded her fingers through his.

"But if you were alone, how would you feel?''

Again she glanced around the street. "Pretty content, I think.''

A line had appeared between Noah's eyebrows. "What if you lived here, had a little apartment, drove a used car, went out with your boyfriend every Saturday night? How would that make you feel?''

She shrugged, puzzled by his question. "I don't know. If that's the life I had chosen, I'd probably be happy.'' Grinning up at him, she added, "Especially if my boyfriend was a handsome horse breeder.''

"I'm serious,'' Noah said as he stepped back. "Is that the kind of life you see for yourself?''

"It doesn't sound like a bad life.'' She still couldn't figure out where he was going with this.

"Not very exciting, either. Not exactly the luxurious life of an heiress.''

She searched his face. "Noah, what's this all about?"

Instead of answering, he asked another question. "Where do you see yourself at the end of the summer, Olivia? Have you made much progress deciding what you want to do?"

The question unsettled her, made her think of endings when she wanted to concentrate on beginnings, the start of something special between her and Noah.

She turned away to face the shop window again. The proprietor was locking up for the evening, shutting off interior lights while leaving a soft, warm glow around the window display. The effect turned the glass into a mirror. Studying her and Noah's reflection, Olivia liked what she saw. Him with his shoulders so broad, his posture so straight and strong. Her at his side. She liked the idea of them together. She suspected the prospect scared Noah to death.

"Why do you want to know what I'm going to do?" she asked. "Is there some reason you want me to leave?"

"I didn't say that."

She faced him again. "Well, that's good. Because I don't want to go anywhere."

"Because you feel safe at the farm?"

"No," she retorted. "Because I feel free. For the first time in my whole life I feel completely free."

He looked unconvinced. "Working on a horse farm for peanuts? Not buying things you want, that you would have purchased in a moment two months ago? That makes you feel free?''

Olivia smiled in response. A warm, contented feeling started in her chest and spread outward. She grinned so hard she giggled. ''Free and happy,'' she assured Noah.

When he shook his head, she reached up and framed his face with her hands. ''I don't know what you're trying to get me to say to you. I only know how I feel. And right now I feel really happy, really content. And more than that...''

She stepped closer, her hands drifting to his chest as she took a long, steadying breath. ''Right now...I know exactly what I want. I want you to take me home and make love to me.''

''Olivia, I thought we agreed—''

''*We* didn't agree on anything. You said, let's wait. Well, maybe I don't want to wait. Why don't I get to choose not to wait?''

She silenced his next protest with a kiss.

All the control and all the logic Noah had used to pull away from her this afternoon melted. Hell, he wanted what she offered. He wanted to feel her satin-soft skin. Taste her pebbling, sweet breasts. Bury his face in the flower-scented glory of her cloud of red curls. He wanted her.

So he silenced the voice inside that preached caution, and he took her home.

Chapter Nine

Almost drunk with desire, Olivia and Noah fell into each other's arms just inside his kitchen door. Deep, scorching kisses punctuated their progress to the staircase. They left a trail. His boots. Her sandals. His shirt and belt. Her sweater. Halfway up the stairs Noah thought he might have to take Olivia then and there. A surge of strength and control helped him pick her up and carry her the rest of the way to his room.

Bright, summer moonlight streamed through the windows. The light turned Olivia's hair to burnished copper, her skin to milk-white. Noah set her on her feet and took a step back in appreciation.

"My God, you look like an angel."

With an artless gesture, as old as womankind, she

pushed a hand slowly through her hair, lifting the tendrils away from her face, then allowing them to drift downward. The movement lifted her full breasts beneath the white lace of her bra. Her gaze never faltering from his, she undid the top button of her skirt and let it fall to the floor. Her panties were a scrap of white, highlighting, rather than concealing, the curve of her hips and the feminine mound at the juncture of her thighs.

Noah's erection nudged insistently against the half-lowered zipper of his khaki slacks. Slowly he drew Olivia toward him. "I've thought about this for what seems like forever."

"Me, too. This is what I want." She lifted her lips for his kiss.

While her mouth opened with gratifying eagerness beneath his, he threaded his hands through her hair. The waterfall of silk was almost as erotic as the press of her near-naked body against his. He passed a new, painful level of arousal. He wanted to take it slow, to savor every inch of her body, kiss every curve, but he was at the limit of his control.

Noah drew Olivia to the edge of the bed and kicked off his pants. His hands weren't quite steady as he reached for the clasp of her bra.

"I'll do it," she whispered, her brown eyes luminous as her gaze met his.

In a moment her breasts were free. They filled his hands, round and firm, the peaks hardening beneath his touch.

Olivia sighed his name, then reached out to touch him. She went very still when her palm encountered the bulge of his erection through the thin material of his boxers.

"Oh," she murmured, drawing away and looking down. Her eyes were big and round when she looked up again. "Oh, my."

Later, Noah realized her expression, a mixture of wonder and fear, should have told him something. At the time, however, all he could think of was getting her beneath him, of finding a home in the nest of curls revealed when he slid her panties down her legs and out of the way. He had the sense to retrieve a condom from a box in the dresser, but most of the next moments were a blur.

He got rid of his boxers. Drew back the bedcovers. Took Olivia down with him. She shuddered as he kissed her breasts and caressed the moist cleft between her thighs. Eyes heavy and slumberous, she watched as he knelt on the bed and sheathed himself in the condom. Her legs parted eagerly as he guided himself into her hot, wet haven.

Sighing in exquisite torture, he pushed forward. She was so small, so tight.

"What the—" Noah's words were cut off by Olivia's groan.

"It's fine," she murmured, pressing her hips upward.

Even as the truth of the moment settled on him, Noah was captured in tight, moist silk. The need to move overtook every other sense. As gently as he could, he pushed into her. Once. Twice. Again and again. She was so tight. So warm. His release was on him before he wanted, before he could begin to build her pleasure. As he spilled himself into her sweet, virgin body, regret mixed with indescribable pleasure.

Though tempted to remain inside her, Noah pulled out and away when the final pulse of his climax had passed. He reached for a tissue from the box on the night table and disposed of the condom. Then he fell back beside Olivia, struggling to catch his breath as he stared up at the ceiling.

Olivia turned onto her side. "Is something wrong?"

Reaching out, he stroked her face. "Why didn't you tell me you were a virgin?"

"Did it matter?"

He faced her, one hand cupping her behind as he drew her tight against him. "Of course it mattered. If I had known, I would have taken some time. I'd have made it right."

"But it was right. It was wonderful."

"But if I'd known—"

Olivia shushed him by placing her fingers against his lips. "If you had known, you would have tried to wait, tried to take control. I wanted this, Noah. I wanted you. I wouldn't change anything. It was perfect."

"If you really think that, then you really were a virgin."

Her laughter rang out, uninhibited and full. Noah was amazed to feel himself stirring against her belly once again.

Olivia giggled. "Is that supposed to happen again so soon?"

"Could be." Noah stroked a hand through her hair. "We'll only do what you want, Olivia. I don't want to hurt you again."

"It didn't hurt." Dark eyes flashing with mischief in the moonlight, she slipped her hand between their bodies and closed her fingers around his thickening shaft.

"That could get you into trouble," Noah said.

"By now you should know that I kind of like trouble."

The stroking motion of her hand made him moan. "This Marshall guy you were supposed to marry really was a loser."

"Why do you say that?"

"You were engaged to him. Didn't you want to sleep with him?"

"Not really."

That admission pleased Noah to no end. Stilling the motion of Olivia's hand, he kissed her. "I'm glad you waited," he murmured. "And maybe now I can make sure you don't regret ending the wait."

He went to the bathroom and returned with a washcloth dampened with warm water. Carefully he bathed between her legs, wiping away any trace of her recent loss of innocence.

Curiously Olivia wasn't embarrassed by the intimate act. She was touched by Noah's thoughtfulness. It felt natural to have him take care of her, to open her body to his touch and his gaze. The warm cloth was soft, his ministrations arousing. Desire welled inside her again. It crystallized when Noah's mouth replaced the cloth and moved against her.

With his lips and his tongue he stroked and licked. He changed her desire into a whirling mass of need. She was drawn deep into a vortex of desire. Then she splintered, her senses falling like leaves in a windstorm.

Before the torrent could give way to calm, Noah filled her again.

Olivia gasped, "Now I know what was missing before."

Then the storm took both of them.

Olivia wakened to sunshine. And something wet and cold. Disoriented for a moment, she turned over and found Puddin' nudging at her shoulder. Her bare shoulder. Which was peeking out of the sheets of Noah's bed. The events of the evening before came flooding back in delicious detail.

Smiling, she snuggled under the covers. Only Puddin's strident bark brought her back to reality.

"All right, all right." Olivia sat up and hugged her pet. "I'm sorry. I know I left you all alone last night."

"Don't worry, I took care of her," Noah said from

the doorway. He was dressed in jeans and an unbuttoned work shirt and held two steaming mugs of coffee. With unshaven jaw and sleep-tousled hair, he looked better than ever to Olivia. She thought of last night in this bed and found herself flushing, all too aware of her nakedness beneath the thin blanket and sheet.

Natural as could be, Noah strolled over to the bed and held out a mug. "I brought her over here about two o'clock this morning. She was one grateful little dog."

"Poor thing." After tucking the sheets firmly under her arms, Olivia took the mug. "Thank you for remembering her."

"No problem." Noah patted Puddin' on the head and was rewarded with a satisfied bark and an adoring canine gaze.

"I think you're beginning to like her," Olivia observed.

"She's grown on me." His blue-eyed gaze centered on Olivia. "Sort of like her mistress."

Flushing again, she smiled at him over her mug. "We're flattered."

He reached out and touched her cheek. "You doing okay this morning?"

"I'm perfect."

Immediately a line appeared between Noah's eyebrows. "Olivia, I want you to know…" The words trailed away as he continued to frown.

"Yes?" she prompted, filled with trepidation.

Looking into her warm, brown eyes, Noah couldn't bring himself to say what he had intended. Last night, when he rescued Puddin' from Olivia's room, he had spent a long time out under the stars, thinking about what he had done. Olivia had trusted him enough to give him her innocence. She had been trusting him all along. When he gave her a ride and offered her a job. When he told her he really needed her help on the farm and with the camp. He hadn't needed her help, hadn't even wanted her around. And he still had that check from her father in his desk.

Her father. God, that was another cause for guilt. Roger Franklin had asked Noah to look after Olivia. What had he done instead? Bedded her. Taken advantage of her inexperience and vulnerability.

But that wasn't the worst of it.

The worst of it was he would do it all again.

"Is something wrong?" Olivia asked.

Noah cleared his throat. Last night out in the backyard with Puddin' he had decided to tell Olivia about the deal he had struck with her father. But now, faced with her sleepy sweetness, he couldn't bring himself to say a word.

He wasn't certain what he feared his honesty would do. Send her packing? What did that matter? She was going to leave sooner or later, wasn't she? When she tired of punishing her father for his overzealous protection, she would return to the life of a princess, a life where she didn't putter in the kitchen or shovel manure. She would return to the life where her clothes didn't come from the discount store and she could buy stained glass that cost ten times the one that had caught her fancy last night. Her father would take her back. Maybe they both would have learned something. However it happened and whatever happened afterward, the fact remained that Olivia would never stay here with Noah. This summer, and he, would be memories before too long.

Except that he would always be her first lover.

Maybe that knowledge was what made Noah keep his mouth shut. Telling her the truth right now would color what had happened between them last night. When Olivia chose to leave, she would do so with this memory untainted.

He cleared his throat again and forced himself to smile. "I was about to ask what you wanted for breakfast."

Olivia's eyes narrowed. "No, you weren't." She set her mug on the nightstand, and, with the sheet held tight against her, got to her knees on the bed. "You wanted to tell me something. What is it?"

"Nothing." He set his mug aside, too, and pulled her toward him. "If you're not hungry..." He leaned down and kissed her shoulder.

"Actually, I am starving," she murmured.

He kissed his way up her neck. "Really?"

"Well..."

His lips closed over hers.

With a groan she let go of the sheet.

Drawing back, Noah took in every inch of her

warm, creamy flesh. "I hope you aren't really starving."

She flushed under his frank appraisal. "Why?"

"Because I intend to keep you in bed a good while longer."

"Don't we have morning chores to do? Horses to feed?"

"They'll live," he muttered as he drew her toward him again.

Puddin', forgotten on the bed, yapped in disapproval. Noah broke away from Olivia long enough to put the dog out of the room and close the door on the canine protests.

He tossed off his shirt as he approached the bed. "We don't want to shock the poor, innocent creature."

Olivia laughed and opened her arms to him.

And in her eager welcome, Noah could put aside all thoughts of telling her about his deal with her father, all thoughts of her leaving. On this beautiful late-June morning, Olivia Franklin was in his arms, and she wasn't going anywhere.

Only later did he begin to ask himself how he might keep her.

Her first night at the farm, Olivia had confessed to Carmen that she had never given much thought to love. Love was meant for people who had choices in their lives, and while still under her father's thumb, she had no choices.

Everything was different now. She was free. Free to be in love with Noah.

The certainty that she loved him didn't hit her all at once. It bloomed day by day. The roots were in her respect for his work ethic, his love for his home and family, his kindness in extending a helping hand to her. Noah had given her a chance to prove she was something more than the spoiled, rich brat he thought her at first. Even his being tough on her had been to her own benefit.

Love grew from her attraction to him, and with the passion he awakened each time they made love. He made her feel confident enough to be bold. She seduced him in the front porch swing late one night. She surprised him in the shower early one morning. She discovered a brand-new use for the kitchen table.

But even more important than respect or passion, Olivia's love bloomed because Noah made her feel she belonged. The day after their first night together, she prepared Sunday dinner, and Carmen and Jordan joined them for the meal. Complimenting her efforts, Noah looped an arm around her shoulders. Such a simple gesture. Yet it signaled to his mother and Jordan the change in his and Olivia's relationship. Carmen and the trainer had beamed their approval. Olivia had felt a sense of family, of closeness, that she had never experienced before. She liked standing at Noah's side, being with him.

As the days sped past and June turned to July, she reveled in these moments of simple togetherness.

When Noah joined her in training the fillies who had become her special project. When everyone worked long into the night painting a backdrop for the skit being planned for the camp. When she joined Noah and Carmen at the front of the eager group of children and adults who gathered for the camp's opening day. When together she and Noah lifted a young boy in leg braces into a saddle atop the gentlest of the farm's mares.

The boy giggled in delight, his face cocked back to catch the sun. Olivia couldn't help thinking of what Noah had told her about his sister's joy at being outside. Surely he was thinking of Charly, and reliving her through this child.

Maybe that was the moment Olivia knew how much she loved him. For as they held on to that boy and exchanged a smile, her heart felt full enough to burst. She was so happy. So incredibly, completely content. For the first time in her life, she felt truly at home.

She realized the feeling didn't come just from loving Noah. She was having a blast with the camp. The kids had responded to her immediately. She thought the silly skit she and Carmen had written had paved the way. Everyone had howled when she came onstage dressed as Dorothy from *The Wizard of Oz* with Puddin' doubling as Toto, and featuring Cody as an amazing giant squirrel with magical powers.

The skit and the first day's art session had got Olivia off to a good start with the twenty-odd children at this first week's session of the camp. Few of the kids groused when the schedule of activities brought them away from the horses for a "cool-down" period in the shed. There, Olivia offered art activities, and Carmen focused on musical games and sing-alongs.

Drawing on her experience with children at the program she had attended in Chicago, Olivia encouraged the kids to use art to get in touch with their feelings. They liked that there was no right or wrong way to express themselves. Smears of paint were as acceptable as carefully crafted self-portraits.

By the end of the fourth day, one of the counselors who had volunteered her services for the camp approached Olivia. "You're a natural with these kids," the woman said. "Carmen told me you're not really trained as a teacher, but you should think about it. Some people just have the gift. You do."

That night Olivia was still bubbling over about the compliment. She, Noah and his mother were at Carmen's house, preparing individual box lunches for tomorrow's session. While a local grocery store contributed all the food, it had to be assembled each night. The volunteer who had been in charge of tomorrow's lunch had been called away by a family emergency. Thus, they were all working after a full day at the camp and around the farm.

As she tucked apples into the brown bags spread across Carmen's table, Olivia was dreaming out loud about going back to school and earning a teacher's certificate. Her flights of fancy carried her even farther, to expanding their camp to last all summer long.

When neither Noah nor Carmen said anything, Olivia demanded, "Can you guys see me as a teacher?"

Carmen looked up from the celery she was smearing with peanut butter for tomorrow's midmorning snack. "It would be wonderful to expand the camp. Having someone young and energetic to help me could make it happen."

Her simple support warmed Olivia. Noah, who was putting sandwiches into plastic bags at the counter, remained silent.

"You look disapproving," Olivia said to him, teasingly. "Don't you think I could cut it as a teacher?"

"Teaching's hard work."

"But rewarding."

"And it pays next to nothing."

"Who cares about that?"

His chuckle held little mirth. "Spoken like someone who's never worried about money."

The bitter undertone in his voice distressed Olivia. "If the work is something you enjoy, is the pay so very important?"

"Of course not," Carmen said with a puzzled glance at her son.

"But most of us have to face reality," Noah continued. "We have to make livings, support families, pay employees."

Olivia protested, "You make it sound as if no one

should consider any profession that doesn't make you rich. Is horse breeding making you rich?''

His gaze sharpened. ''I think you're well aware that it is not.''

''But you love what you do. I think I could love teaching. Why shouldn't I consider it?''

''A teacher's salary might be hard to swallow for someone who is used to having money.''

Setting down the two apples she held, Olivia glared at him. ''Please remember that I have not had money, as you put it, for almost two months.''

''Two whole months.'' Noah dropped a sandwich in a bag and sealed it shut with a fast, economical motion. ''Wow.''

''Why are you being so sarcastic?'' Olivia demanded.

He didn't even look up at her. ''I'm simply pointing out that teaching won't put you back in the lifestyle you left behind at your father's.''

''I don't want to go back there.''

''Not yet, anyway,'' he muttered, half to himself.

Before Olivia could protest again, Carmen spoke up. ''Much as I'd love to listen to the two of you squabble, I'm tired and we've got a full day ahead tomorrow.''

Olivia clamped her lips shut on her angry words. For all the wonderful qualities Noah possessed, he could also be incredibly smug and knowing at times. He thought he knew best for everyone. Hell, if she had let him control the pace, they might still be circling each other like two curious animals.

Genuinely ticked off at him, she finished sorting apples, picked up Puddin' and left Noah and his mother to finish the lunches.

Carmen turned to her son the moment Olivia was gone. "What was that all about?"

"Just the truth," Noah said as he dropped sandwiches and bags of chips into the paper sacks. "Being a teacher would never satisfy Olivia."

"And why are you so certain of that?"

"Come on, Mom. A week at our little camp is fun, but she could never do this day in and day out."

"I did it. I don't think she's any less smart or capable than I was."

"She wasn't raised to work."

"She hates being useless. She wants direction in her life." His mother cocked her head to the side as she studied Noah. "These last few weeks, I've been thinking she's found that direction with you."

Noah ignored her and completed his task. "These are finished. Anything else you need me to do?"

She continued looking at him with the same sort of probing gaze that had elicited hundreds of confessions from him as a boy. It didn't work this time. He wasn't prepared to share his feelings and fears about Olivia with anyone.

Carmen sighed. "You're not asking for my opinion, but I'm giving it."

"Mom—"

''Don't let your ego ruin this with Olivia before it has a chance.''

He stared at her in consternation. ''My ego? What does that mean?''

''Well, Mr. *Know-It-All,* it means you should listen to Olivia and respond to what she says and does, not what you expect her to say or do.''

Noah grunted. ''You and Jordan sound like a broken record with your advice.''

''Maybe that's because we know how hardheaded and prideful you can be. We were here when you chased Amy off.''

''Chased Amy off?'' Stunned, Noah braced his hands on his hips. ''Are you forgetting she left me at the altar?''

''I haven't forgotten a thing.'' Carmen screwed on the lid of a half-gallon jar of peanut butter with more force than necessary. ''What I remember most was how you refused to even talk to Amy about her father buying the farm. You got angry and defensive and you laid down the law. You weren't going to sell and that was that.''

''Don't tell me you wanted me to sell?''

''Of course not,'' his mother retorted with a scowl. ''This isn't about you selling or not, and I'm certainly not sorry you didn't marry Amy. She wasn't right for you. But I also know you didn't listen to that girl. You never heard anything she said about what she wanted from life. Your mind was made up about what she was and what she wanted and what you wanted from her.''

"That isn't—''

"Please just be quiet and listen,'' she said, speaking with a parental authority she hadn't exerted with him since he was a teenager. "You were bullheaded about Amy, and it cost you in the end. I don't agree with the way she handled things by just not showing up at the wedding, but I also wonder if she thought she had a choice. By that time I'm sure she knew she'd get nowhere by trying to have a discussion with you.''

"You make me sound like a damn fool.''

"Not a fool. Just someone who retreats from the truth when they feel their status quo is threatened.''

Noah forced a laugh past the anger burning in his chest. "I don't know what you mean.''

"When everything started turning sour with Amy, you avoided facing the possibility that you two weren't meant to be together. Now you're going in the opposite direction, refusing to see that Olivia could be exactly right for you.''

With an emphatic shake of his head, he said, "She is not right for me. Nor am I for her.''

"Then why are you involved with her?''

"Excuse me, Mom, but is that really any of your business? We're adults.''

"You're very much in love with her,'' Carmen said, her tone gentling. "You love her, and because you think she'll run out on you, just as Amy did, just as so many people have left you, you're scared to death.''

Noah had to get out of here. "This is crazy, Mom. I don't want to argue with you about Olivia. In a few months she won't even be here.''

"Why? Are you determined to chase her away?'' Carmen asked, sadness in her expression.

He left before she could say more.

But she was so right. He was such a fool. He had fallen in love with Olivia. Fallen in love with a princess, when he had nothing to offer her but debts and dreams.

He was so angry with himself. It was stupid of him to have lost control of this situation. Every day with Olivia pulled him deeper in trouble. Having her here every day made him wish for a future that was only a false hope. That's why he had snapped at her tonight. Hearing her talk about teaching and expanding the camp had been physically painful. He knew none of it would ever happen.

In the kitchen of his house, he found Olivia scrubbing pots from dinner with a vengeance. For some reason the sight of her in suds up to her elbows, her jeans torn and her face weary, made him angrier than ever.

"I told you I would do those," he said.

"It's my turn," she retorted.

"But you worked all day at the camp."

"So did you."

"I'm used to working all day."

She glared at him over her shoulder. "In case you've forgotten, I've been doing some pretty hard work around here for a while, myself."

"That's why I suggested you let me do the dishes."

In response she turned the water on full blast and returned to her scrubbing.

"Come on, Olivia. You're dead on your feet. What are you trying to prove?"

"I'm simply washing the dishes."

He raised his voice to be heard over the running water. "You don't have to. You don't have anything to prove to me, and your father's not even here."

She pivoted to glare at Noah. "What's my father got to do with anything?"

"You took this job to show him something. That doesn't mean you have to be on duty every minute."

"On duty?"

Swearing, Noah crossed the room and turned off the water. "I wish you'd just go to bed and let me do this."

"Am I not doing something right?"

"Olivia—"

She dropped the pot into the sink with a splash. "For goodness sake, if I'm not washing the dishes up to your standards, then just tell me."

"That isn't what I'm saying. Hell, I'm trying to be nice and do something for you."

"No, you're trying to tell me what to do, and I don't like it."

''Fine.'' Noah flipped the water back on, full force. ''Go right ahead. You want to wash the dishes, then wash them.''

He stalked off, fully aware he had made a jackass of himself over something as petty as dishwashing.

In about two minutes Olivia appeared in the doorway to the den, demanding to know what was really wrong.

Looking up from the newspaper he had been pretending to read, Noah took a deep breath. God, he felt so ridiculous. He hated what getting involved with her had done to him. Yet what could he do? Lay his heart on the line to Olivia, tell her he loved her? Or maybe show her the check from her father. That would end things for sure.

He would sooner risk a stallion's hoof to the head than do either of those things at this moment.

''Why are you so angry with me?'' Hands on her hips, Olivia glared at him. ''What did I do?''

You were born, he wanted to say. You climbed into my truck with your sassy smile and your curtain of red hair and you captured my heart. And fool that I am I keep hoping against hope that this will turn out to be real.

Laying the paper aside, Noah pushed himself out of his chair. ''Sit here.'' He directed Olivia to a nearby chair. ''I have something for you.''

Returning just moments later from the closet in the hall, he carried a large package, wrapped in brown and gold paper. "This is for you," he said, propping it next to her chair.

She blinked in surprise. "What in the world?"

"Open it and see."

Hesitantly, still frowning, Olivia tore away the paper to reveal the stained glass she had admired so much on their evening in Franklin. For a moment she simply stared at it. Then she looked up at Noah in confusion.

"Is it not the right one?" he asked, concerned. "It's the sunflower."

"Yes, it's the right one. It's...lovely." As she stared at the beautiful design, Olivia couldn't help thinking about the price tag. Hundreds of dollars.

"You don't seem excited."

"I'm stunned."

"Do you like it?"

"I love it, but..." She couldn't help herself. She had to ask. "Why give it to me?"

"Because you wanted it."

"But, Noah, this cost far too much."

"I wanted to give you something, to thank you for all your hard work."

"Do you give Jordan and Cody gifts like this?"

His face hardened. "I think you'll agree that our relationship is a little different from the one I share with either of them."

"Yes, of course, but..." Olivia realized she was being horribly ungracious. Noah wanted to give her a gift. He was a practical man. He wouldn't have spent more money than he could afford. Why was she acting this way?

The answer was simple. The gift felt like something her father would do. Whenever they had argued, or she had tried one of her escape routines, he bought her a present. Something obscenely expensive. Usually jewelry. She had grown to hate his way of trying to make up to her with things.

It was wrong of her to compare that with this gift from Noah. After all, he had bought this before he knew they would argue tonight. He had bought it to thank her, to show his appreciation and perhaps, his affection.

"I'm sorry," she murmured as she stood and hugged him. "It's a beautiful gift. I love it."

He hugged her back. "I can go hang it in your room right now."

"But I'm always here. Let's put it here." She went over and pulled the curtain back from the window that overlooked the side yard. "The afternoon sun will catch it every day."

Noah hesitated.

"You don't think it will fit?"

"Of course." Noah hefted the panel and crossed the room to place it in the window, propped in place. He turned to Olivia. "We don't even have to hang it, so if you want it moved..."

A few moments passed before Olivia realized what he meant. They could prop it in the window, temporarily, until she left. He expected her to leave.

Mumbling an excuse, Olivia gathered up the discarded wrapping paper and retreated to the kitchen once again. She thought she smiled at Noah, but she couldn't be sure. Her head was reeling. She felt sick at her stomach.

He didn't expect her to stay.

She wasn't sure why that knowledge shocked her so. He had never, ever said anything about loving her. He never proposed anything permanent. Just because she loved him didn't mean anything about his feelings.

No wonder he had gotten all testy tonight at Carmen's when Olivia had been prattling on about making the camp a summer-long event in the future. He was probably wondering where she got the idea she was invited to enlarge *their* camp.

Olivia didn't realize she was standing over the trash can where she had stowed the wrapping paper until Noah spoke. "Hey, are you okay?"

"Just tired."

He crossed the room and reached out to rub her shoulders. "The camp is wearing you out."

"It's not that," she murmured.

"You should take tomorrow off."

Gaze snapping up to meet his, she took a step backward. "What in the world for?"

"You're tired. You can have the day off."

"And leave Carmen and you and the others to cope, when I've promised I'll be there? No way."

"I think you need the time off."

"Are you telling me I can't work at the camp tomorrow?"

"No, but—"

"Then stop it." Her voice rose in impatience. "I don't need time off or special treatment. No one else around here gets that. Why should I?"

Noah raised his hands and then let them fall to his sides. "You know something, I think we're both tired and we shouldn't have this conversation right now."

"You think? What about what I think?"

"Olivia—"

"Stop talking to me like I'm a child."

Face coloring with anger, Noah shook his head. "I'm not going to talk to you at all when you're this upset."

Her hands fisted at her sides. "You sound so damn much like my father. It makes me sick."

His color deepened. "You're being hysterical."

"That's exactly what he would say when he couldn't control my every word or deed."

"Just stop it." Noah turned away from her. "I'm going to bed. You can do whatever you want."

Olivia wanted to stop herself from speaking, but she couldn't. "Just tell me one thing before you go, Noah. One thing. Do you love me at all?"

He whipped around to face her, shock registering in every feature.

She swallowed past the lump of fear in her throat. "I asked if you love me. Because I love you. What do you think of that?"

Chapter Ten

She said she loved him.

What did he think of that?

Olivia's bold statement and even bolder question hit Noah like a strong, one-two punch. In those first reeling moments of trying to absorb her words, he felt a strange burst of joy.

She loved him. How did he feel?

He wanted to say he was wonderful, fantastic, the happiest man in the world. If he truly believed her, that's exactly what he would say.

Only he didn't believe her.

To his relief his voice was steady as he answered her. "You don't love me, Olivia."

Her face flushed scarlet. "What?"

"You're confusing sex with love. I'm the first man you've made love with. I'm your first serious relationship. This summer is your first taste of freedom. You don't love me."

She squeezed her eyes shut and swayed a little. She swatted Noah's hands away when he reached for her.

"Everyone experiments this way, Olivia. Your father kept you closed off from possibilities when you would have been trying your wings. That's all this is."

"You're insulting me, acting as if I'm too stupid to know my own feelings."

"Olivia, please. Just calm down. You're tired and you're angry with me because I've been a jackass tonight. I admit I've been…all out of sorts. But that's my problem, not yours. You're saying things you don't really believe."

She opened her eyes to glare at him. "Why do you get to decide all of this for me? Why do you know everything I think or feel?"

Reminded uncomfortably of the lectures about ego and pride he had received from Jordan and his mother, Noah took a moment to think. They had told him to listen to Olivia, to hear what she told him. He understood what they meant. But he also understood Olivia better than either of them.

He knew how low she had been when she walked away from her father in Texas. He knew she had been determined to prove herself capable of making her own decisions. She had been ripe to try anything, despite her vulnerability and innocence. He had disregarded her state of mind and plunged into a relationship he knew couldn't last. Of course she thought she loved him. But that was now. He knew what would come later.

She was clearly struggling to hold back tears as she faced him. "I guess this answers my question about whether or not you love me, doesn't it?"

He wanted, desperately, to hold her, but he knew she wouldn't allow him to touch her. "Olivia, I'm not trying to hurt you. I'm trying to save us both some anguish in the future."

"What does that mean?"

He shoved a hand through his hair and gestured to the kitchen. "Hell, Princess, take a look around. This isn't your world."

"Meaning it's yours, and I'm not welcome."

"Meaning you belong to the manor, and this is the servants' quarters."

She waved that aside. "Stop with the poor, pitiful me routine. You may not be rich, but you're far from a pauper. And besides, I don't give a damn. I'm not like Amy. I'm not asking you to sell out to my father. I don't want anything we can't find right here."

"Not now, anyway."

Hands held out, she stepped toward him. "Why are you saying all this? I thought I had proven to you that I'm not some rich little brat, only interested in money and things. If that's who I was, I never would have left my father."

"You haven't been gone that long, Olivia. You don't know how you're going to feel next week or next month. You may very well want to go home."

"I can't go back there."

"Your father will take you back."

"Whether he will or not isn't the point. What I'm trying to say is I can't ever lose my freedom again. That means more to me than anything his money can buy. I've learned more about myself since coming here than ever before. I finally know exactly who I am and what I want." The muscles worked in her throat as she swallowed. "I want you, Noah. Just you."

Noah didn't doubt she meant everything she was saying. But Amy had said she loved him, too. Hell, Owen had made a hundred different promises, as well. To his mother. To him. Noah had believed them. Neither of them had come through in the end. Why should he trust Olivia to be any different?

He shook his head. "I understand why you can't see the truth right now, Olivia, but you don't love me."

She stepped even closer to him. "I'll show you. I'll prove it."

"Olivia, there's no reason for you to try and prove anything to anyone. You are who you are. I am who I am. There's no future for us, no matter what."

She got right up in his face. "I don't believe you. I don't think you can look at me and say you want what we have to end."

Fearing she was right, he closed his eyes. "I don't want to take tests or play games."

"Just say it, Noah. Say you want me out of here. Say it and I'll go."

He couldn't. Hard as he tried, he couldn't make the words come out.

Olivia made a soft sound of triumph.

Looking at her again, Noah cut her off. "Just because I don't want you to go doesn't mean I think any differently about our future."

"I'll show you that you're wrong. I can prove how right things can be between us. I'll prove that I belong here with you."

Olivia felt more than a little crazy. A little desperate. Those feelings colored the kiss she offered to Noah. He resisted, as she had expected. He wasn't about to give her any encouragement. Not when he was bound and determined that they didn't belong together.

But she kept on kissing him, and he began to relent. With an agonized groan, he caught her up in his arms. She could feel the rock-hard evidence of his arousal and felt a thrill of triumph.

Against his lips, she murmured. "See? You want me."

"It's sex," he said as his hands roamed over her body. "Just sizzle, baby. Someday you'll realize that's all it is."

She went cold. She stilled in his arms and pushed herself away.

Noah had a tense, knowing glint in his blue eyes. "See? See how fast it can burn out?"

If this had been two months ago, Olivia suspected she would have thrown something at him. She used to slam things around when she couldn't get her way with her father. Like a child pitching temper tantrums. But she wasn't that child any longer. In fact, she felt about a hundred years old as she faced Noah in this kitchen where they had laughed and loved together.

With a last, sad sigh, Noah turned and left her standing there.

Puddin' was at Olivia's feet, her black button eyes riveted on her mistress. With stiff, mechanical motions, Olivia picked her up and left for her room over the garage. All her things were here, but she couldn't stay in this house. Not tonight. Not until she could get her thoughts together.

Inside the hot, shabby room, moths stirred around the overhead light. The heavy song of insects pressed in from the outdoors, the sound so maddening that Olivia shut it out quickly with the noisy, old air conditioner.

She put Puddin' down on the bed, then flopped beside her, much as she had done her first night in this room. She had been so determined that night, set on proving herself to everyone. She had wanted to make it without running back to her father for help. She had wanted to show Noah what she was made of.

Two months later had she proven anything to anyone?

Oh, she could shovel horse manure, clean tack, drag herself up at 5:00 a.m. in order to check the dressings on a lame yearling. She understood the finer points of training a Tennessee Walking Horse in the famous rocking-chair gait worthy of a show ring. She could bake a pan of corn bread and a cherry pie to rival Carmen's. She had experienced the pure joy of a child who couldn't walk set free to move on the back of a powerful horse.

Most of all she had learned how to love a man with all of her heart and soul.

She had learned so much, but none of it was good enough for Noah. He didn't believe she was any different from the bride on the run he had found in his camper.

What could she do to prove herself? *What?*

The urgent questions made her sit up on the bed. She realized that for weeks now she hadn't been trying to prove anything to anyone but herself. She had stopped caring whether Noah appreciated anything she did. Oh, she was happy when he liked something, but her world didn't hinge on his approval. Moreover, she couldn't remember the last time she had worried what her father would think about her sticking with the menial, exhausting farmwork.

Everything she had done, everything she had learned, had benefited her. No matter what happened with Noah, no matter if she ever spoke to her father again, she was stronger for having gone through this summer. For the first time in her entire life, she believed in herself. She honestly thought she could formulate a plan and carry it through without having to depend on someone else.

She felt...*strong*.

Olivia realized that was an odd sensation for a woman who had just learned the man she loved didn't love her. But considering who she had been two months ago, there was genuine victory in feeling this way. She was strong enough to get through anything. Even losing Noah.

"Okay, guys, are we ready to visit the horses this morning?"

At Carmen's invitation the day campers let out a chorus of cheers, and the usual morning exodus began from the camp's main gathering at the shed. The children moved down the ramp and the smoothly graded path to the stables by various means. Some in wheelchairs propelled themselves. Others were pushed. Many walked, aided by braces, crutches, parents or counselors.

Each morning the children were assigned simple chores with the horses. Those who were able assisted with feed and cleaning the stalls. Others curried the coats of the gentlest horses. Still others were seated on mounts right away and began their joyous rides under the close supervision of adults.

Spirits were mixed today, Olivia observed. For

these kids, this was their last day of camp. On Monday a new group would arrive for a week of activities. Olivia had her own reasons for feeling sad, and knowing she wouldn't see these children again anytime soon only added to her melancholy.

The little boy she was escorting down the path was the same one she and Noah had assisted onto a horse together the first day of camp. His name was Samuel, and he was an eight-year-old handful. A spinal cord injury during a car accident when Samuel was three had affected his legs. The doctors had feared paralysis, but as Samuel's mother had explained to Olivia, the boy had pushed himself to recover. He was able to walk with his braces and crutches, and he could actually move pretty fast.

Samuel adored the horses, had progressed from a gentle nag to one of Noah's stallions. If allowed, he would have ridden all day. He wasn't alone in that desire, and that was one reason Olivia wished the camp could be expanded.

As they approached the stables, she saw Noah with the stallion he called his finest, Smoky's Delight. The typical Walking Horse is not a huge animal, but Smoky was larger than normal. Black and somewhat intimidating to the kids at first, Smoky actually had a calm temperament that had born up well during the first week of the day camp.

Olivia forced herself to look at Noah. She had been dreading this moment, wondering how she would feel. But nothing had changed. Her heart quickened and eagerness tightened her chest.

He looked straight at her, gaze unwavering, chin proudly raised. Like the animal whose bridle he held, Noah was the picture of masculine confidence. No doubt he was feeling righteous this morning, certain of the wisdom of what he had decided for both of them.

Usually Olivia appreciated his assurance. Right now she wanted to wipe that stoic expression from his face.

Turning away from him, she looked down at Samuel. ''Looks like your favorite mount is saddled and ready this morning.''

''Smoky!'' Pulling his hand away, Samuel started toward Noah and the stallion before Olivia could react. The boy knew better than to approach any of the horses this way, but he was more excited than usual, given that this was his last day at camp.

''Slow down,'' Olivia called as Samuel darted forward, faster than she expected, his braces flashing in the morning sun.

Maybe it was her call that bothered Smoky. Or perhaps both of them racing toward him. But whatever the cause, the normally controlled animal was spooked. He jerked his reins from Noah's grasp and reared.

Olivia's mouth went dry as the stallion's hooves pawed the air over Samuel, who was falling back in fear. She caught the boy, stumbled and felt the *whoosh* of wind as the horse set his powerful legs down.

Noah saw Olivia and the boy fall and lived the longest moment of his life as he fought to reclaim Smoky's reins. The horse came down a good foot away from Samuel and Olivia, but it was too close for comfort. Way too close for Noah's heart.

He was too busy hanging on to his horse to do anything for Olivia. The most important thing was to get the excited stallion away from the children and adults who came swarming forward to offer their help. Through the crush, however, his terrified gaze connected with Olivia's.

Inside the nearby paddock, Noah handed the reins off to Jordan. Then he pushed his way to where his mother and Olivia were kneeling beside tearful young Samuel.

"Hey, now," Noah said, stroking the boy's dark, tousled hair. "You're all right, aren't you, big guy? You're not hurt."

"He's fine," Carmen said. "Just scared."

Fighting the tears that streamed down his face, Samuel looked up at Noah. "I didn't mean to scare Smoky. You know I didn't mean it."

"Of course not," he assured the boy.

"He just got excited," Olivia said.

"And got away from you," Noah observed, fury roughening his voice.

She sat back on her haunches and stared at him.

"It was an accident," Carmen said, darting a look

between them. "Just an accident, and no one's hurt." Taking Samuel by the hand, she stood to reassure everyone else. She and the counselors began herding everyone toward the stable where they belonged.

Noah stood, and noticed Olivia's wince as she also got to her feet.

"You're hurt," he said, taking her by the arm.

She jerked away. "I skinned my knee."

A jagged tear in her jeans revealed a nasty scrape.

"Come on." Again Noah took her by the arm and marched her through the crowd and down the stable foyer to his office.

Once the door closed behind them, she pulled away from him again. "You don't have to manhandle me."

"I hope you realize you or that boy could have been seriously hurt."

"Of course I know that," she shot back at him. "I don't need you to tell me what's obvious."

He opened a drawer in his desk and pulled out a first aid kit. "These kids are our responsibility."

"It was an accident. It could have happened to anyone."

He pried open the kit. "I knew you were tired. I knew you should have just taken the day off. You're upset and angry with me. You shouldn't be here today."

"Shouldn't be here at all. Isn't that what you mean to say?" Olivia demanded, two flags of angry color appearing in her cheeks.

He chose to ignore that comment. "Just sit down. Let me see to that knee."

"There's nothing wrong with my knee. It's you that's the problem."

"Olivia, I know your knee is hurting."

"The all-powerful Noah Raybourne knows everything, of course."

"Let me doctor your damned knee," he commanded again.

Her back braced against the door, she didn't move. "If this were anyone other than me, they wouldn't have been accused of letting Samuel get away. You would call what happened just an accident, which it was. But because it's me, this becomes a big problem. Poor, fumbling Olivia, she can't do anything."

"I saw you and the boy go down and my heart stopped." Noah slammed the kit down on the desk. "How do you expect me to react?"

"Like something other than a madman."

Turning away from her, toward the window, he drew in a long, cleansing breath, then released it, trying to calm his still-racing nerves. "All right," he muttered, turning back to her. "I'm okay now. Let me fix your knee."

Olivia shook her head. Her brown eyes were cool as she studied him. "Anyone who didn't know better would think you cared about me."

"Of course I ca-care." Noah was annoyed by the way his voice broke on the word.

She regarded him quietly for a moment longer.

"You care, but you don't have any faith in me, do you?"

He refused to answer.

"I realized last night that I haven't proved anything at all to you about myself. You still think I'm the same person who hid in your camper. You don't see that I've changed."

"Of course I see that."

"No," she insisted. "You don't. You can't separate me from everyone else who has ever let you down. To you I'm the same as Amy, who also had a rich father and who broke your heart. I'm a princess who needs to be treated with kid gloves, pampered and protected."

She paused to draw in a ragged breath. "The bottom line is you don't respect me enough to believe I know my own mind."

"Respect isn't the issue." Noah came around the desk, stopping just inches from her. His blue eyes swept her from head to toe. "The truth is written all over you, Olivia. You don't belong here."

He took one of her hands in his and held it up for both of their inspection. In place of the soft, well-manicured hands she had brought to the ranch, her nails were now clipped short and unpolished. The back of one hand sported a blister from popping bacon grease. One finger was encased in a brightly patterned children's bandage. Her palms were stained from paints at the camp.

Noah glanced up at her. "Just look at your hands,

Olivia. Look what two months here has done to your hands.''

Her eyebrows drew together as she followed his gaze. ''I like the way these hands look. I like knowing the horses they've fed, the dirt they've turned over in the garden, the food they've prepared. These aren't empty, useless hands connected to an empty, useless brain. That's how I felt before I came here. These hands have shown me that I don't want to be a helpless, pampered socialite ever again. I'd rather dig weeds beside your mother or guide one of your horses through its paces than ever go back to the way I was.''

Her voice began to tremble. ''I don't understand why you can't believe me or respect me. You have to know how much I respect you. You helped me, gave me a chance. Aside from everything else, that means so much.''

Closing his senses to her soft entreaty, Noah continued to shake his head. She had romanticized these last two months. Staying here would be a different story. Suddenly he wanted it over with. He wanted her gone for good. And he knew exactly how to accomplish that.

''There's something you need to realize, Olivia.'' He stalked around his desk, fumbled with his keys and pulled open a drawer. With only the slightest hesitation, he withdrew the check from Olivia's father and threw it on the desk. ''Look at that.''

Olivia recognized the handwriting before she could

even process what the check said. But when the names and the amount clicked into place, a pain started in her chest. She looked to Noah for an explanation other than what seemed obvious.

His face was hard and tight and closed. "Your father paid me to give you this job, Olivia. Paid me to look after you this summer."

Look after her? Is that all he had been doing?

"In addition to this check, I get another one if you stay here all summer. Plus, I get Royal Pleasure."

Still holding the check, she eased down in the chair beside the desk and tried to take it all in. "Why...why haven't you cashed the check?"

He looked away, toward the family pictures grouped on the far wall. "I figured I'd do that when the job was complete."

The job. She was a job. Noah, whom she had thought so special, so principled, was just another one of the "suits."

Olivia tried to feel the pain this revelation should bring. She tried to feel anything other than the awful, cold emptiness that had enveloped her. So the job he had offered had been engineered by her father. In return for helping her, Noah got money and the horse he wanted free of charge. Once again she had been a commodity, a bargaining chip between her father and a man. In the end was that all she was worth?

Mechanically Olivia rubbed her forehead as she gazed out at the green pasture beyond Noah's window. She could see the children, mounted on horses, being led single file by counselors and volunteers across the edge of the field. Moments ticked past. Slow, agonizingly silent moments.

Finally she cleared her throat. She speared Noah with her gaze. "Are you going to charge my father extra for sleeping with me? Or will that earn him a discount?"

Noah's features contorted as he moved toward her. In her haste to move away, Olivia knocked over her chair. She backed toward the door. She was ashamed for feeling sorry for Noah, for hating the despair now etched in his features. She didn't want to feel anything but anger.

Where the hell was the anger? Why didn't it come?

She scrambled out of the office before she got her answer. Staying near Noah was impossible to bear.

In the foyer children called to her. Counselors smiled and asked if she was okay. Olivia mumbled some excuse about her knee. She had to get out of here. She had to get to the house, get her things together, collect Puddin' and get away from this farm. As far away as she could. As quickly as she could.

She was about to stride out of the stable and into the sunlight when a familiar voice called her name. Carmen. *God, what was she going to tell Carmen?*

The older woman strode up to her, tall and slim in her camp T-shirt and drawstring khaki slacks. "Are you all right, dear?"

The sweet concern in her voice made Olivia want

to cry. But she summoned all her composure. "Of course."

"Noah shouldn't have blamed you."

Olivia wanted to tell Noah's mother that there were a great many things he shouldn't have done. She didn't have the heart, however.

"I'm going to the house for a few moments, I need—" Her throat closed up, and she had to force her voice to work. "I need to get something."

Though Carmen frowned, she said nothing.

Once again Olivia started forward. After two steps Samuel waylaid her, his eyes big and round and solemn. He wanted to apologize again for spooking Smoky. He needed reassurance. So Olivia gave it.

A counselor called out to her next, to help one of their shyest, most physically challenged campers, who was proudly stroking a curry brush across the coat of a placid, chestnut mare.

Next it was a volunteer. Another camper. A parent.

Everywhere Olivia turned, someone asked for her help. She gave up on trying to leave. She gave herself over to the questions, the demands and the needs she could serve.

The hands Noah had seemed to think were ruined reached out again and again. To soothe and comfort, to lift and carry. The lips that had felt frozen found their smile once more. The hollowness inside her filled up with the children's laughter. The chill around her heart melted with their hugs.

The camp day wound forward. The only thing

missing was Noah's presence. He was nowhere to be found. Cody went searching when children asked for him, but reported his truck was gone. Otherwise, it was the normal hectic whirl. Olivia filled every moment, drawing strength from the work and those around her. From them a certainty grew inside her, an answer to the question of her self-worth.

Yes, she was more than a bargaining tool for her father.

She was more than a means to a financial end for Noah.

She was worth much more than either of those men gave her credit for. She could see her worth in the faces of these children. She could feel her worth in the joy she felt by helping them.

By the end of the day, after the last, tearful good-byes had been said, Olivia felt strong once more.

In the open end of the camp shed, she and Carmen stood and stared at the dust settling on the now-empty driveway.

The older woman heaved a sigh. "I hated seeing them go."

Olivia slipped an arm around her waist. "I know what you mean."

Carmen turned to her with a smile, then lightly touched a hand to Olivia's cheek. "You've made this year very special."

The idea Olivia had first given voice to last night bubbled up again. "I wish they could each have two weeks here. I'd like to see the camp expanded."

"It's a wonderful idea, but the funding is so difficult. Even though so many people volunteer their time
and donate supplies, there's some transportation to
consider. The insurance is the worst part. We have to
make provisions for something unforeseen happening,
something like what could have happened to you and
Samuel this morning."

"I know a lot of rich people."

"Aren't all of those people you've left behind?"

"I'd go to them for the right reasons. For this
camp, I'll even go to my father."

Carmen's blue eyes, so like Noah's, were sharp and
considering as she studied Olivia. "You've been upset all day. Do you want to tell me about it?"

There was no putting this off. "Noah and I
are…well, we're over."

Hesitating only a moment, Carmen gave her another hug. "I'm sorry, dear. Maybe it's just—"

"No." Olivia cut her off. "He's made himself
pretty clear about me." She didn't want to go into all
the details. Carmen was Noah's mother. He could tell
her what he wanted. All Olivia was concerned with
right now were her own plans.

"I want to stay for the rest of the summer," she
continued. "I want to be here for the camp next week.
Then I want to make plans for some weekend sessions
this fall. I'll start making calls about the funding tonight. How does that sound to you?"

"My dear, if you can find the money, I'm game."

"But this is Noah's farm. His horses. He might not want—"

"He'll want this," Carmen assured her. "He would do anything in remembrance of Charly."

Olivia nodded, trying to reconcile the man who had been such a devoted and patient brother with the man who had taken that check from her father.

"I think Noah expects me to leave," she cautioned Carmen.

"Then you can stay with me."

"I won't come between the two of you."

"Don't you worry about that." With a weary sigh Carmen cast a gaze about the messy shed. "I suppose we should get this place ready for Monday morning."

"We could do it tomorrow," Olivia suggested.

With a laugh, Carmen held out her hand. "Come on, then. Let's go to my house and collapse. Something tells me you could use a little downtime."

Olivia agreed with the woman. Only there was something she had to do first.

At Carmen's house she went straight for the phone and punched in a familiar number. When the phone was answered on the other end, she hesitated only briefly. Then, her voice strong, she identified herself to her father's secretary. Almost immediately she was punched through, and Roger Franklin's voice poured through the line.

"Ready to come home?" he asked.

Olivia forced herself to laugh. "Not hardly." She

took a deep breath and lied, "I called to thank you for asking Noah to give me a job."

"So he told you about that, did he?"

"Yes, he did."

Her father chuckled. "I figured he would. Raybourne didn't strike me as someone who would keep that from you for long."

Though she almost wished he had kept it from her forever, Olivia agreed. Then she changed the subject. "I have something here that I'd like your help on."

"My help?" Again he laughed. "I didn't think you needed me for anything."

Listening to his laughter, Olivia also heard a note of strain. "What's wrong?" she challenged. "Are you sorry I was able to fly once I escaped the nest?"

He sighed. His words came slowly. "No, I'm not sorry."

Olivia was surprised into speechlessness.

His tone heavy, her father continued, "I've missed you, Olivia."

She didn't know if she bought that. "I'm sure you've been keeping very close tabs on me."

"That's not the same as you being here."

"Where you could orchestrate my every movement?"

He paused once more. "That's not why I missed you."

She held the phone, wishing with all her heart that her absence had made a real, emotional impact on him.

"The house has seemed empty," he continued. Then he laughed. "I kept looking around for that dog of yours."

"I'm not coming home," Olivia said, fearful that his sentimental act was part of a scheme to lure her back to the fold.

He surprised her again. "I know you're not."

When she found her voice, she said, "But there is something I need from you."

"Okay."

"It's something important. Something I really believe in."

"Oh?"

Olivia could almost imagine her father settling back in his chair. She hoped that he, unlike Noah, would believe enough in the changes in her to give serious consideration to her plea for help for the camp.

"I'm listening," her father prompted.

She began to tell him about the camp.

The dew was heavy on the thick green grass as Noah guided Royal Pleasure across the pasture. A glance at the sun hovering round and yellow just at the treetops told him it would be another late-July scorcher. Already he could feel the heat and humidity working its way under his shirt.

Beneath him, Royal Pleasure moved with the easy, rocking gait he knew so well. She was a queen, this horse. She represented so many of his dreams. He had wanted her so much. Too much, he realized now.

He eased her into a walk and turned back toward the stables. Only when he approached the neat, white fence that connected to the building did he see the figure perched on the top rung.

Olivia waited for him, Puddin' cradled in her arms.

He had been dreading this moment ever since she pushed her way out of his office yesterday. Hell, he had left the place rather than face her. For the rest of his life, he thought he would see her wounded eyes and hear her small, hurt voice when she asked him if her father had paid him to sleep with her. Hearing that part of their relationship reduced to the level of stud service had driven a stake through him. But he had deserved the question. He deserved whatever she thought of him.

He had half expected her to be gone when he returned last night. The lights burning in her room over the garage showed she had stayed.

But she needed to go. He had taken steps to see that she left.

His mouth went dry as he slipped from Pleasure's back and led her toward the fence.

''She's a beautiful horse.'' Olivia's face was set, her voice calm. ''I understand why you wanted her.''

''You know the reasons I wanted her,'' Noah murmured. ''I was trying to get back what my stepfather lost.''

''I understand,'' Olivia repeated. ''Really, I do.''

Noah looked at the ground. Whether she understood or not didn't matter. What mattered was the deception he had carried out in order to get Pleasure. He should have driven away from the deal Roger Franklin offered. Then none of them would have been hurt.

"I've asked your father to take Pleasure back," he told her. "He's considering it."

"Why?" Olivia demanded. "You're going to earn the horse. I'm staying here. At least for the rest of the summer."

Noah shook his head. "No, you're not."

Her expression hardened into stubborn lines. "I'm staying. You'll earn all your money and your horse."

He couldn't believe what he was hearing. Why would she want to stay? "No matter what, I wouldn't take anything from your father now."

"After all that's happened, why not?" she demanded. "You made a deal with him. Take what's yours."

"No, I can't do that now."

"But—" Olivia broke off her protest. Shading her eyes, she looked up and said, "What's that sound?"

Noah followed the direction of her gaze. Only now was he aware of a faint buzzing sound in the distance. He had barely processed the noise when a speck appeared over the ridge beyond the farm.

"That's a helicopter," Olivia said.

"Probably your father."

"What?" Her voice squeaked. "Why would you say that?"

"Because I called him last night to come and get you."

Fury exploded in her voice. "You what?"

"I figured you would want to go home."

Before Noah could react, Olivia slipped from the fence, balled up her fist and punched him right in the gut.

Chapter Eleven

Noah doubled over in pain. "What the hell was that for?"

"For being such a high-handed jerk! You had no right to call my father." Olivia's words were punctuated by the sound of the approaching helicopter and Puddin's frantic barks.

Holding on to the reins of Pleasure, who was becoming agitated by the noise, Noah said, "I knew you'd want to get away from here, and I couldn't very well send you off in a horse trailer again."

"You idiot." Olivia let loose with one of the most colorful and profane curses she had learned from Jordan. All the anger she hadn't been able to feel toward Noah yesterday spilled over now. "You make me sick. If I were in my right mind, I would leave here."

"Your chance is coming," Noah shouted back.

Conversation was impossible as the copter began to descend onto the pasture. Olivia was glad. She knew she wouldn't be responsible for what she would say. She wanted to punch Noah again. Far from being ashamed of being moved to physical violence, she wished there was something nearby that she could use to bash him in the head.

Instead, all she could do was wait for her father's helicopter to settle on the ground. A "suit" stepped out first, then her father climbed out and jogged across the pasture, waving for all the world like this was some sort of social call.

"What in the hell are you doing here?" Olivia shouted over the copter's fading engine.

Her father's grin didn't slip a millimeter. "Is that any way to snap at your dear old dad?" He patted Puddin' on the head and was rewarded with a deep-throated growl. Roger looked surprised. "Looks like both of you grew some teeth this summer."

Noah was still subduing Pleasure. Roger made a quick gesture and one of the "suits" took over the horse.

Roger slipped off his sunglasses and peered from Olivia to Noah and back again. "I figured I'd better get out here and see what was going on. First Olivia calls me—"

Noah interrupted him by demanding of her, "You called him?"

"Not that it's any of your concern, but yes."

"But you punched me for doing it."

"That was different. You had no right—"

"Hold it," Roger cut in smoothly, holding up a hand. "The point is that both of you called." He looked at Olivia. "Raybourne said you wanted to come home, but since that's not what you told me, I thought I should come check this out."

"Noah was wrong," Olivia said, glaring at Noah. "He wants me to go, but I'm not going to do it."

Noah began, "Why the hell would you stay?"

"Because I want to," she retorted.

"So why did you call your father?"

Roger cut their argument off again. "Olivia phoned me just a few hours before you called, Raybourne. She wanted some money. For the camp."

"Your mother and I are expanding," Olivia told Noah. "My father was the best source of money I could think of."

Her father sighed. "Nice to know how you regard me, Daughter."

"Tell me why I should regard you in any other way," she demanded. "All these years you've kept me a virtual prisoner. You were willing to trade me in marriage to your protégé."

"Marshall is a good man."

"Who was more interested in becoming president of the company than in me." She drew in a ragged breath. "That wedding proved what I had begun to suspect. You don't love me. You just want to control me."

Roger fell back a step. Something Olivia could only describe as pain shot across his face. "You know that's not true. I loved you too much. That's why I—" he faltered "—I made some mistakes. But not because I didn't love you. After your mother was…taken, I was afraid for you. I realized when you ran away from the wedding that I had gone overboard. That's why I let you go. My God, letting you walk away from me in that East Texas jailhouse was pure torture. Leaving you here was harder than you can imagine."

"Why?" Olivia asked, sarcasm heavy. "You hired a new goon to look after me."

"A goon?" Noah said. "So now I'm a goon?"

"Among other things," she shot back.

"I wanted you safe," her father interjected. "I had a feeling Raybourne could keep you safe."

In the awkward silence that fell after that statement, Noah felt shame sweep over him. Instead of protecting Olivia, he had used her. She had become a bargaining point in a business deal, exactly the situation she had run away from when she escaped her wedding. Then, instead of being smart and sensible, he had given in to his own feelings and become involved with her. In the end he had hurt her.

His gaze locked with Olivia's. Voice low, he said, "I'm sorry. I let you down."

To her father he said, "The horse is yours, Franklin. Like I told you last night, I don't want her." He dug in his jeans pocket and came up with the man's creased and folded check. "Here's your money. I don't want that, either." He ripped the check in two and let both halves fall to the ground.

Then he walked away.

Staring after his straight, proud back, anger fell away from Olivia. Yearning ate at her, instead. God, she hated this. She hated loving him despite everything.

"Aren't you going after him?"

With a start, she turned to see her father watching her. She stiffened. "Of course not."

"It could be a mistake. Go after him."

"Stop it," she ordered. "Please just stop telling me what to do. I can make my own decisions. You may not think I can. That stubborn jackass may not think so, either, but I'm capable of deciding what I want to do."

A new expression came over her father's florid features. A look she had never encountered before. She thought it might be approval.

"I think you are capable of doing anything you want," said Roger.

"And what's caused this sudden change of mind?" she demanded.

"You walked away. You proved you didn't need me. When you didn't come home after the first few weeks I knew you weren't going to. I had people watching this place—"

"I should have known."

He held up a soothing hand. "I just wanted to

know you were really safe. What I found out was that you would rather scrub out stables than come home to me...." Regret shone in his eyes. "While you were gone, I finally realized how unhappy you must have been. How unhappy I had made you. Knowing that you felt you had to run away really disturbed me."

"I didn't think you'd ever let me go. And I couldn't marry Marshall. I didn't love him."

"I know that now. I've realized..." Roger cleared his throat. "I tried to rob you of the happiness your mother and I knew together. I thought I had your best interests at heart, but now I know...well, I know I was wrong. That's not easy for me to say."

"And that's the understatement of the century," Olivia replied, emotion coming through in her voice.

He reached out and touched her arm. Quietly, he said, "Do you love that man, Olivia?"

"Why? Are you going to try and buy him for me?"

"I don't think he's for sale," Roger answered. "I don't think he ever really was. If he was, he would have cashed that check."

Hope began to flutter in Olivia's chest.

"Do you love him?" her father asked again.

As Noah disappeared into the barn, Olivia's eyes filled with tears. "Yes," she murmured. "I do."

Roger took Puddin' from her arms. "This isn't an order, Olivia. This is a suggestion. Go after him."

She hesitated only a moment more before she ran into the stable.

Noah was in his office, staring out the window. He

didn't even turn when Olivia stepped into the room. He jumped when she said his name. Then he simply stared at her.

"Can't we—" she took a calming breath "—can't we do something about this mess?"

He remained silent.

She stepped forward. "I don't want to leave here, Noah. Whether you believe me or not, I love you."

Noah closed his eyes, unable to bear her bright, shining face. "Go away, Olivia. Maybe someday this summer will be a nice memory for you. Just like someday you'll find a man who deserves you."

"Does anyone deserve a rich little screwup who causes trouble everywhere she goes?"

He looked at her again. "That's not who you are. Much as I wanted to keep thinking it was, that's not you. You're beautiful. Caring. You...embrace life." His voice began to break. "Just your smile changes the whole world."

"If you think that of me, then why can't you see that I love you, that I want to be here with you?"

He released a sigh. "I gave up believing I deserved anything as special as you a long time ago."

"I'm not anyone else, Noah. I'm me. And I'm here. Just say the word and I'll never leave. There isn't any other place I want to be."

God, he wanted to believe her. He had never wanted to trust anyone the way he wanted to trust her at this moment.

She came around the desk and took his hands. Her

brown eyes were shining, brimming with tears. "I just want to be at your side, Noah. Give me your trust and your love, and I don't need anything else."

The sincerity and honesty in her face, in her simple words, broke through the last barrier inside of Noah. He couldn't resist. Despite all the evidence he had gathered to the contrary in his life, he still had to believe in love. He had to trust her.

With a groan he took her in his arms. His hands went to her hair as he murmured, "I love you, Princess. I can't help myself. I love you with all my heart."

He tasted tears on her lips. Then her laughter was bubbling over, robust and throaty, filling his very soul.

From the doorway came a furious bark. Then an admonition to hush.

Turning in Noah's sweet embrace, Olivia found her father holding a furious, yapping Puddin'. Carmen was at his side, smiling through tears. Cody and Jordan were lurking in the corridor, peering over their shoulders.

"Olivia's going to marry me," Noah announced.

She whirled around to face him again. "You didn't ask me that."

He flushed. "But I thought. I just assumed you would—"

"We've still got to work on that dictatorial manner of yours," Olivia said. "It'll be a good project for the honeymoon."

Grinning, Noah kissed her nose. "I promise to try."

Her father set Puddin' on the floor and pulled a slender calendar from his pocket. "Now, about the wedding. Three months from now will fit into my schedule pretty well."

"This wedding is going to fit *my* schedule," Olivia said.

Frowning, Roger flipped through the pages of the calendar again. "But there's the Japanese deal and a trip to Russia and..."

"Just get out," Olivia ordered, laughing. "Carmen, take my father to your place and feed him something delicious. We'll be over in a few minutes."

The door closed on a protesting Roger.

Olivia slipped back into the arms of the man she loved, the man who loved her. "About the wedding," she said. "How does next week sound?"

"Like a good plan, Princess."

She wrinkled her nose. "I really hate that nickname, you know."

"Then how about this one?" Noah's blue eyes crinkled. "Mrs. Raybourne. It has a good ring to it, don't you think?"

"Absolutely."

As they sealed the deal with a kiss, Puddin' barked her approval.

*   *   *   *   *

▼™ SILHOUETTE®
SPECIAL EDITION™

AVAILABLE FROM 21ST DECEMBER 2001

JUST EIGHT MONTHS OLD… Tori Carrington

That's My Baby!

Chad Hogan had given Hannah McGee a sports car instead of an engagement ring—big mistake! Now their passion burns brighter than ever, but Hannah has a baby girl attached to her hip and she's playing hard to get!

THE TYCOON'S INSTANT DAUGHTER
Christine Rimmer

The Stockwells

Ruthless in business and in love Cord Stockwell always got what he wanted, and he wanted his baby *and* the sexy temporary nanny. He'd even *marry* her to make sure of it!

MAN WITH A MISSION Lindsay McKenna

Morgan's Mercenaries

While on a mission to rescue his sister, tower of testosterone Captain Jake Travers needed a guide, but he got much more in Lieutenant *Ana Lucia* Cortina…

THE RANCHER NEXT DOOR Susan Mallery

Lone Star Canyon

Jack Darby had been Katie Fitzgerald's childhood hero, her forbidden teenage love. But now they were both older and wiser—*old enough to control who they loved?*

PRETEND ENGAGEMENT Tracy Sinclair

Swept up into an Italian fantasy, Jillian Colby was amazed when a handsome Italian duke came to her rescue and agreed to pretend to be her fiancé. But was it true *amore?*

HER MYSTERIOUS HOUSEGUEST Jane Toombs

Tall, dark and mysterious Mikel arrived out of nowhere, and with her haunted past Rachel couldn't risk trusting anyone, least of all a sensual stranger who seemed to be a man on a mission!

SILHOUETTE® SUPERROMANCE™

is proud to present

nine months later

Friends... Lovers... Strangers...
These couples' lives are about to change
radically as they become parents-to-be

HER BEST FRIEND'S BABY
CJ Carmichael
January

THE PULL OF THE MOON
Darlene Graham
February

EXPECTATIONS
Brenda Novak
March

THE FOURTH CHILD
CJ Carmichael
April

Join us every month throughout the
whole of 2002 for one of these dramatic,
involving, emotional books.

SILHOUETTE® SPECIAL EDITION™

is proud to present

The Stockwells

Where family secrets, scandalous pasts and unexpected love wreak havoc on the lives of the rich and infamous Stockwells!

THE TYCOON'S INSTANT DAUGHTER
Christine Rimmer
January

SEVEN MONTHS AND COUNTING...
Myrna Temte
February

HER UNFORGETTABLE FIANCÉ
Allison Leigh
March

THE MILLIONAIRE AND THE MUM
Patricia Kay
April

THE CATTLEMAN AND THE VIRGIN HEIRESS
Jackie Merritt
May

1201/SH/LC24

Available from 19th October 2001

Winter
L O V I N G

TWO HEART-WARMING LOVE STORIES

FROM

DIANA PALMER
JOAN HOHL

FREE

2 BOOKS
AND A SURPRISE GIFT!

We would like to take this opportunity to thank you for reading this Silhouette® book by offering you the chance to take TWO more specially selected titles from the Special Edition™ series absolutely FREE! We're also making this offer to introduce you to the benefits of the Reader Service™—

★ FREE home delivery   ★ FREE gifts and competitions
★ FREE monthly Newsletter   ★ Exclusive Reader Service discount
★ Books available before they're in the shops

Accepting these FREE books and gift places you under no obligation to buy; you may cancel at any time, even after receiving your free shipment. Simply complete your details below and return the entire page to the address below. **You don't even need a stamp!**

YES! Please send me 2 free Special Edition books and a surprise gift. I understand that unless you hear from me, I will receive 4 superb new titles every month for just £2.80 each, postage and packing free. I am under no obligation to purchase any books and may cancel my subscription at any time. The free books and gift will be mine to keep in any case.

EIZEC

Ms/Mrs/Miss/Mr ....Initials............................
BLOCK CAPITALS PLEASE

Surname..

Address..

....

....Postcode ....

Send this whole page to:
UK: FREEPOST CN81, Croydon, CR9 3WZ
EIRE: PO Box 4546, Kilcock, County Kildare (stamp required)